"I AM
NOT YOUR BROTHER!"

His voice was husky with his effort to keep its volume down. "What is it going to take to get it through your head that we are not related?"

"But—" How could he say that? They were too.

Whit read her thoughts before she could speak them.

"It means nothing that my father married your mother. There's no blood tie between us. You aren't my sister. You're a woman, and a damned beautiful woman at that!"

She couldn't deal with this kind of talk— not from Whit. She tried to push away from him, but he simply tightened his hold to bring her closer to the bare wall of his chest.

THE
LANCASTER MEN

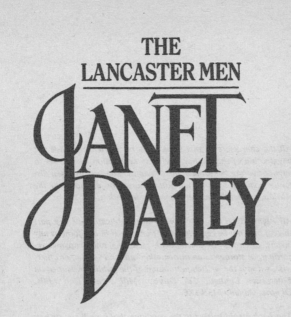

JANET DAILEY

Harlequin Books

TORONTO • NEW YORK • LONDON
AMSTERDAM • PARIS • SYDNEY • HAMBURG
STOCKHOLM • ATHENS • TOKYO • MILAN

First published by Silhouette Books 1981

ISBN 0-373-15190-X

© *Janet Dailey 1981*

® *are Trademarks registered in the United States Patent and Trademark Office and in other countries.*

Printed in U.S.A.

THE
LANCASTER MEN

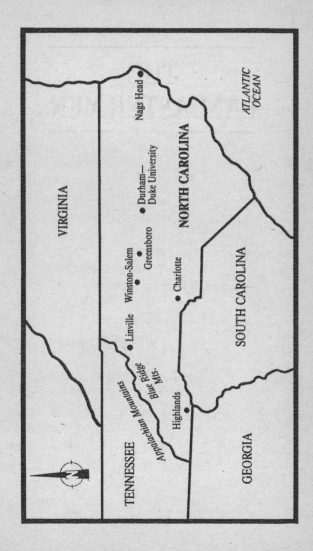

CHAPTER ONE

WHEN A family of tourists drifted on to view other contests of the Highland Games, a space was left on the inside ring of spectators. Shari Sutherland quickly slipped into the vacated area, drawing her two friends with her. Her hair glistened blackly in the afternoon sun, thick and full-bodied as its loose waves brushed her shoulders.

Her attire differed slightly from that of her female companions. Her slacks were camel tan, topped with a silk blouse in the palest shade of cream. Around her neck, she wore the tartan scarf of the Sutherland clan.

The brown-haired Beth Daniels wore snug-fitting gold-colored jeans and a matching checked blouse with the tails knotted at the waist while her chic, blonde counterpart, Doré Evans, was dressed in white slacks and a shimmering striped blouse in variegated shades of turquoise and lavender. Neither of

Shari's friends displayed the distinctive plaid of a Scottish clan.

The Grandfather Mountain Highland Games were held each summer in MacRae Meadows located high on the slopes of the mountain which gave the annual event its name. The festivities attracted a throng of spectators and participants alike to this North Carolina area that so resembled the rugged terrain of Scotland.

The proud, boisterous wail of the bagpipe filled the air, issuing forth its wild cry that sang through the blood. Shari felt the power of its music and her green eyes were alive with the heady strength of it as she watched the competing dancers.

Without taking her eyes from the contestants, she leaned toward her two friends to whisper an explanation. "This is the *Ghillie Callum,* the Sword Dance."

"You could have fooled me," Doré murmured dryly, a little aloof and unmoved by the spectacle. Shari was used to the faintly patronizing attitude of her friend and smiled away the remark without taking offense.

"Malcolm Canmore of Scotland is the one who is usually given credit for originating the dance,'' Shari continued in the same low voice. ''After a battle in 1054 in which he killed one of Macbeth's chiefs near Dunsinane, he took his dead enemy's sword and laid his own over the top of it to form a cross. Then he danced over the symbol to celebrate his triumph.''

''It's kinda like a war dance, isn't it?'' A trace of irony slanted Beth's mouth. ''Society accepted this, but thought the dances of the American Indian were strange and heathen.''

''You're right. This was essentially a war dance.'' Shari addressed her remarks to Beth who seemed to be more in tune with the imagery of the dance than Doré. ''Like the Indian war dances, it was performed on the eve of a battle. It was a way of relieving tension and displaying self-control as well as a means of foretelling the outcome of a battle.''

Beth pulled her glance away from the competition long enough to cast a puzzled frown at her friend and guide. ''How could a dance predict the outcome?''

''The warrior would dance over his sword and scabbard, arranged in the shape of a cross. If his feet didn't touch the sword or scabbard, they would be victorious in battle. But if he misstepped and disturbed the position of the sword or scabbard, it was considered an omen of defeat,'' Shari explained.

''These dancers aren't doing it right,'' Doré pointed out. ''They aren't using a sword and a scabbard. Those crosses are formed by two swords.'' Which proved she had been listening despite her expression of disinterest in the proceedings and Shari's explanation of the dance's origin.

''For the purposes of modern dance, two swords are used.'' Shari assured her friend that it was being performed correctly. ''The displacement of the swords with a missed step is now a means of eliminating contestants from the competition, so, in a sense, it is still a bad omen.''

''It certainly is for the dancer,'' Beth agreed, a smile of amusement flashing across her face.

A responding smile curved Shari's bow-shaped mouth as she lapsed into silence, her explanation concluded, leaving her free to watch the intricate pattern of precise footwork. The dance demanded grace and energy, the arms arched above the head, the quick action of pointed toes flirting close to the crossed blades.

In the background, the bagpipe established the fevered pitch, sending tongues of excitement through Shari's veins with its battle song. Her own feet ached to take part in the ancient ritual, but she held them still. When the last note of the song faded to a wheezing sound, she turned from the scene with a trace of regret.

"Where can we get something cold to drink?" Doré's glance swept the horde of spectators with a look of long-suffering patience. "Isn't anybody else as thirsty as I am?"

"I wouldn't mind a cold drink," Beth appeared to feel obligated by friendship to agree with the blonde. "There were some vendors by the entrance, weren't there, Shari?"

"I believe so, yes. We'll work our way in that direction and see," she suggested.

She knew better than to suggest that Doré might satisfy her thirst at one of the water fountains located conveniently nearby. Doré had an almost continental aversion to water as a drink.

Their place on the inside ring of spectators was quickly taken by other tourists as they moved away. The crowd that had gathered for the Highland Games was a colorful mixture. Male and female alike were garbed in the individual tartan plaid of their particular clan, the men in kilts and the women in pleated skirts.

Since the public was invited to attend the festivities, there was a bright array of summerwear along with the traditional dress of the Scots. Athletic competitions were being held in addition to the dance and piping contests.

"I don't know when I've seen so many men with knobby knees," Doré remarked after they had passed a particularly portly gentleman with his kilt flapping about his knees. "What are those funny little leather pouches hanging from their waists?"

"They are called *'sporrans.'* The *sporran* is a kind of belt purse," Shari explained. "You have to remember when these costumes were common attire, pockets were not in vogue, and men needed to carry their small possessions in something. A more ornamental *sporran,* made from fur, is used with eveningwear and the plain leather is considered proper for daytime.''

"It's really quite unusual and decorative.'' Doré was always the first to wear new fashion trends. "I'm surprised it hasn't caught on.''

"You could always start a new fad,'' Beth suggested.

"I might do that.'' It was a shrugging reply that seemed to indicate the suggestion would be forgotten tomorrow.

They circled a small group of people all wearing the same tartan plaid. Beth slowed to glance back at them, then turned to Shari with a thoughtful frown. "None of those people look like they're related to one another. I know this is known as the Gathering of the Scottish Clan, but I'm not sure that I know exactly what a 'clan' is. Do they just share the same last name?''

"*Clan* is Gaelic for family. Essentially this is a series of family reunions to which the public is invited,'' Shari explained. "While they may not be directly related, they've traced their family genealogy and learned that they share a common ancestor. This celebration is really a means of preserving our Scottish heritage.''

"But why here in this particular place in North Carolina?'' Doré swept the locale with a surveying glance, not overly impressed. "It's very picturesque, but . . .''

"Do you have the feeling, Shari, that our city friend is more comfortable surrounded by concrete than trees?'' Beth teased.

Shari laughed briefly, but let that question pass. "Probably the most basic reason for this site is because the originators of the celebration were raised here in Linville. But there were other contributing factors as well. When North Carolina was being colonized, a lot of Scottish families settled here in the Blue Ridge Mountains. Plus the area bears a very strong resemblance to the Highlands in Scotland. In that sense, this was a natural choice.''

"I suppose,'' Doré conceded as her attention was claimed by the sight of a vendor's stall. "Good. That man is selling soft drinks.''

After they had bought their cold drinks, they searched until they found a shady spot to sip them away from the crowds. Shari lifted her gaze to the mountain that silently watched over the celebration.

Grandfather Mountain, so named by the Indians because the broken outline of the mountain peak looked like the profile of an old man gazing skyward. It had become one of the more popular recreation sites in the State with its swinging footbridge providing a view of nearly one hundred miles, its cave of inlaid stone, and a natural rock likeness of the Sphinx.

So many of her summers had been spent in the shadow of this mountain that seeing it again was like seeing an old friend. She remembered the times when she and Rory had hurried to keep up with Whit while they hiked the mountain's trails.

Rory had always been so impatient whenever she stopped to gaze at the rhododendron growing in wild profusion on the slopes, but not Whit. Whit was the one who pointed out the rowan tree and the sand myrtle.

A smile flitted across her lips as she recalled the time she and Rory had taken off on their own. A mist had swept in through the mountain gaps and covered the top of Grandfather Mountain. She and Rory had gotten lost in it, but Whit had found them. It was the first and only time that she could recall ever seeing Whit angry and he had been furious with them.

"Why the smile?" Beth inquired with a curious look.

Shari lifted a shoulder in a dismissing shrug. "I was just recalling some of my childhood 'misadventures.'" She didn't bore them with the details.

"Do you live very far from here?" Doré stirred the ice in her drink with a straw. "I know you said the condominium where we're staying is just a summer place."

"Gold Leaf is over an hour's drive from here, out of the mountains," she replied, still thoughtful and vaguely reminiscing. "The Lancasters used to own one of those old summer houses in the village when I was a child. It's cooler here in the mountains and we'd spend the hot, summer weeks here instead of at the farm. The summer house was sold a few years ago. Then Whit bought the condominium."

"What is Gold Leaf?" Beth wanted to know.

Doré supplied the answer before Shari could. "That's the name of the family tobacco plantation," she said, revealing her interest in anything that implied money.

"The Lancaster family made its money in tobacco. That's why they named the farm Gold Leaf," Shari explained. "In recent years, it has diversified, raising other crops but tobacco is still one of the principal ones."

"Does your family live there?" Beth questioned. "You said it belonged to the Lancaster family."

"It does. My mother lives there and my younger brother, Rory, as well as Whit who runs Gold Leaf now since Grandfather Lancaster isn't able to get around any more," Shari replied and finished her cold drink.

"Then your mother was a Lancaster?" Beth attempted to figure out Shari's relationship to the Lancasters.

"No. The explanation is a little involved," she smiled. "My father was Robert Sutherland. He was killed in a car wreck when I was only a couple of months old. I was a year old when my mother met and married John Lancaster who was a widower with a twelve-year-old son. My younger brother, Rory, is actually my half brother. And Whit is my stepbrother. There isn't any true blood relationship between myself and Granddad Lancaster." Shari glanced at Beth. The brown-haired girl was frowning intently. "I've confused you, haven't I?" she laughed.

"I don't think so." Beth shook her head, but she didn't appear too certain. "What about your stepfather John Lancaster?"

"He died when I was fourteen from pneumonia complications. At the time, Whit was already being groomed to take his place in the family business. He stepped in to fill the void after my stepfather died and managed the farm under the direction of Granddad Lancaster. Granddad put him in full charge of the operation three years ago and ostensibly retired." While he didn't run the business anymore, Shari knew full well that Granddad Lancaster still ran the family.

"How old is your grandfather?" There was a wistful note in Beth's voice. Knowing how close she was to her own family, Shari guessed her friend was feeling a twinge of homesickness.

The question made her pause to add up the years. The resulting answer made her realize that she had forgotten her step-grandfather was that old.

"He's seventy-eight, but he looks like he's in his sixties. He's still very much the patriarch of the family." A face she knew all too well.

"Since we're so close, you are planning to visit them, aren't you?" Beth frowned, because Shari hadn't mentioned anything about it.

Smiling lightly, Shari tried to shrug away the twinge of guilty conscience. "When we planned this vacation, I thought it was supposed to be a complete break from everything for us. Besides, it would hardly be fair for me to visit my family when neither of you can see yours since they are so far away."

"I don't mind," Beth assured her.

"I think it would be fascinating to see your family home," Doré inserted. Until that moment, Shari had believed her blonde-haired friend would be an ally.

With pressure being applied from both sides, Shari attempted to delicately explain her situation at home. "I don't think either of you understand what you're saying. Twenty minutes after we arrive at Gold Leaf, you'll probably find yourselves referees in a shouting match."

"Why?" A frown of puzzled concern took over Beth's expression.

"To put it mildly, I don't get along very well with my grandfather." There was a rueful twist of her mouth since her reply was something of an understatement. "We can't carry on a conversation for five minutes without an argument starting. Granddad Lancaster has some antiquated notions about a woman's role in life and he disapproves of just about everything I do."

"I suppose he's one of those old-fashioned Southern men who believes that women are the weaker sex and need to be looked after and protected." Doré read between the lines of Shari's answer and made a mocking conclusion. "No doubt, he has the attitude that educating a woman is a waste of time."

"He is sufficiently liberated to concede that education is a good thing, but he doesn't like my choice of university or my major." Her sense of fair play wouldn't permit her to go along with such a sweeping condemnation of her step-grandfather's attitude.

"What's wrong with Duke University?" Beth's expression was ringed with disbelief, her college pride aroused. "Heavens, it's one of the top colleges in the country."

"But there are several others in the State that are equal academically," Shari reasoned, a hint of a smile curving her lips. "As far as Granddad is concerned, Duke has several drawbacks. Number one, I can't live at home while I'm attending college." Her green eyes widened in mock horror. "And Heaven only knows what could happen to a young girl living on campus—away from the nest and without the sheltering wing of the family to protect her from lecherous college boys always ready to take advantage of her."

"Do you mean it isn't like that?" Doré feigned surprise and they all laughed.

A trace of amusement remained in Shari's voice when she continued, "Naturally he feels I should study something in the Arts or Domestic Sciences. He can't see any value in chemistry. His biggest complaint against Duke is too many 'outsiders' are enrolled there."

"Outsiders?" Beth frowned. "What does he mean by that?"

"Students from outside the State of North Carolina," Shari explained. "Granddad is

convinced I'll end up marrying one of them
and move away. He insists I'll never be happy
if I leave.'' Although she didn't admit it, she
thought he could be right about that. She did
love this wild and proud land.

"How did you ever manage to persuade
him to let you enroll at Duke when he feels so
intensely about it?'' Doré questioned.

"I didn't persuade him.'' She shook her
head.

"I suppose your mother did,'' Beth
guessed.

"No.'' Shari laughed at the suggestion that
her mother would oppose an edict of Frederick Lancaster. "As far as my mother is concerned, his word is law. Besides, nothing
would make her happier than keeping me and
Rory at her side forever. She doesn't believe in
untying the apron strings.''

"Then how did you manage to come to
Duke?'' Doré eyed her narrowly, trying to
understand.

"I guess you could say that I literally ran
away from home,'' she shrugged to make light
of the difficult decision. "One afternoon
when no one was home, I packed all my
things and left a note, telling them where I

was going. Luckily I didn't have to rely on them for financial support. When I turned eighteen, I was able to have control of the small inheritance my father, Robert Sutherland, left me. Between it and my scholarship grant, I'm able to pay for my own education."

"Your grandfather must have been upset when he read your note." Beth's sympathies seemed to be with Shari's grandfather.

"That's putting it mildly." Shari grimaced. "He was furious. He came after me, determined to take me back home. We practically had a knock-down, drag-out fight right there on campus. But I was legally of age so there really wasn't anything he could do. He couldn't force me to go home. Then he filled my mother's head with so much nonsense that she came to get me, all upset and worried. It was harder trying to deal with her tears than with Granddad's rage."

"What happened?" Beth asked, then immediately explained her question. "I mean, I know you're attending Duke University so they didn't make you leave, but did your grandfather finally become reconciled to your choice?"

"Not hardly," she sighed grimly. "After I'd been attending classes for about a month, I went home for a long weekend to try to smooth things out. It was a three-day, continuous argument. When I left, I swore I would never come back." She laughed, remembering her impassioned declaration.

"Oh, Shari, you didn't!" Beth breathed in alarm.

"I did," she nodded and smiled. "Of course, that didn't last. At the start of the Thanksgiving break, Whit arrived, packed my suitcases, and dragged me home."

"Whit is your stepbrother?" Doré arched an eyebrow in Shari's direction to be certain she was correct in her assumption.

"Yes." Shari paused thoughtfully. "At times, Whit can be just as ruthless as his grandfather, with one major difference. Whit doesn't argue."

"Does he approve of what you're doing?" Doré asked.

"No, he doesn't think I needed to leave home to attend college, but he does agree that it was *my* decision to make, not anyone else's," she replied.

"You really think a lot of your step-brother, don't you?" Beth observed and turned to Doré, not giving Shari a chance to respond immediately. "Have you noticed the way her face lights up when she talks about him?"

"Whit is one of a kind," Shari stated as if that explained it all.

"What makes him so special?" Doré challenged.

Shari had never had to describe him to anyone before. She suddenly didn't know where to start. "He's tall and good-looking in an austere kind of way. His hair is dark brown, but he spends so much time in the sun that it has streaks of dark gold. And his eyes are an unusual amber-brown color. When he's angry, they look real dark and hard. Then other times, they sparkle with gold. He's intelligent and has a marvelous sense of humor."

"He sounds fascinating," Doré murmured with more than a little feminine interest.

But Shari didn't catch that note of aroused female curiosity for a member of the opposite sex. She was too caught up in her attempt to give her friends a clear picture of her stepbrother, something she'd never had to put into words before.

"I know you two would like him," she insisted confidently. "At times, he can be positively infuriating but generally he's always willing to listen to what you have to say, no matter how trivial. His shoulder is always available to cry on. And it always seems like he's there when you need him most." She paused for a minute as it occurred to her the best way to sum up her description. "Whit is every girl's ideal image of what a big brother should be like."

"I don't know about you, Beth," Doré arched a glance at the brown-haired girl, "but I was under the impression she was describing the ideal *lover* instead of a brother."

Stunned by the suggestion, Shari laughed shortly. "Don't be silly."

Just for an instant, her imagination took over and she had a clear, mental picture of Whit taking her into his arms in a loverlike embrace. She shied away from the sudden and unexpected race of her pulse, blocking out the image.

"I'm not being silly," Doré insisted. "It's a pity you couldn't hear yourself when you were describing him—or see the look on your face. You appeared much more interested in him as a man than as your brother. From all you said, I don't blame you a bit. I'd love to meet him."

There was something avidly feline about Doré's look that reminded Shari of a cat ready to stalk its prey. She found herself bristling at the thought of her friend sinking her claws into Whit. Even more startling, she felt an almost territorial claim on him and the hostile sensation that her friend was trespassing on private property.

It was unsettling to learn she could feel jealousy over him. Disrupted by that, Shari was hesitant to examine the emotional ties that had always bound her so close to him.

"Is he married?" Doré inquired.

"No." It occurred to her that she had always found something to dislike about every girl Whit had dated through the years.

Even now it seemed inconceivable that he might marry, yet it was perfectly logical to assume that he would. Whit was a very virile man. It was only natural for him to want a woman with whom he could share his life. Until that moment, Shari had never thought about Whit in terms of what his sexual and emotional needs might be. In so many ways, she had taken him for granted.

"We are going to have to meet this stepbrother of yours, aren't we, Beth?" Doré enlisted her friend's support.

"Well, I definitely think we should pay a visit to Shari's family since we are this close," Beth agreed to that extent. "How would you ever explain to them why we didn't stop to say 'hello'?"

"It's very easy." Shari tried to let her irritation rise at the way they were ganging up on her. "They don't know we're here."

"But surely you told them?" Beth stared.

"I wrote Mother that I was going to be spending these two weeks with friends. I didn't mention where. I'm sure she'll assume that I'm spending it with one of your families," she replied.

"But the condominium? Don't they know we're using it?" Beth protested.

"No. In mother's last letter, she said they weren't going to be able to get away to spend any time here this summer. Since none of the family was going to be using it, I thought it was the ideal place for us to come." Shari didn't see what Beth was getting so upset about.

"Do you mean we're staying here without permission?" Her friend frowned and bit worriedly at her lip.

"We don't need permission to stay here," Shari explained patiently. "The condo belongs to Whit. He certainly isn't going to object to us using it."

"I agree with Beth. I think you should have let him know we were going to be here," Doré stated. "It could be embarrassing if he decided to come here this weekend with a female companion."

"Whit wouldn't do that sort of thing," Shari retorted.

"Any man would do that sort of thing," Doré corrected with a knowing look. "That's probably why he has the condominium, so he could have a weekend hideaway."

"It's used for the family as a vacation spot," she insisted. The thought of it being used for any other purpose was distasteful. "If you two have finished with your drinks, I'd like to watch some of the athletic events being held."

"If you insist," Doré agreed with ill grace.

CHAPTER TWO

THE AFTERNOON crowd was just beginning to disperse when the three girls left MacRae meadows to return to the Lancaster condominium so they all would have time to shower and change before going out to dinner at the country club's restaurant. The resort complex was almost literally carved out of a forest of trees and rock near the sheer cliffs of Grandfather Mountain.

When Shari inserted the key into the door, she discovered it was unlocked. She glanced over her shoulders at her two friends, her expression puzzled. "I locked the door before we left, didn't I?"

"I thought you did," Beth agreed, but she didn't sound positive.

Turning the knob, Shari pushed the door open and looked inside before entering. Nothing appeared to be out of place. She was just about convinced she had left the apartment without locking it until Doré called her attention to the suitcase sitting at the foot of the stairs.

"I have the feeling we aren't the only ones who decided to use the condominium this weekend," she murmured.

Shari tried very hard not to remember Doré's earlier suggestion that Whit used the place for romantic weekends, but she felt an indignant anger begin to grow. She started toward the stairs leading to the upstairs bedrooms.

"Hello? Is anybody here?" She called out.

She had one foot on the stairs when a voice answered her. Only it came from the direction of the kitchen. "Shari? Is that you?"

She pivoted in surprise. She recognized the voice, but it wasn't the one she had expected to hear. The kitchen door was pushed open and a tall, young man walked through. His hair was as black as her own, but his eyes were dark brown instead of green.

"Hi, Sis." He didn't seem at all surprised to see her. "How come you haven't stocked this place with some food? The cupboards are bare or haven't you noticed?"

"Rory! What are you doing here?" She stared at her younger brother and recovered her shock to move forward to meet him.

"I could ask you the same question," he retorted with a grin. "I thought I was going to have the place to myself until I went upstairs and saw all those suitcases filled with women's clothes. I was almost convinced that I was in the wrong condo. Then I saw your name on one of the luggage tags. Nobody mentioned to me that you were going to be here this weekend."

"I didn't tell them," she admitted, then came back to her original question. "You still haven't told me what you're doing here. Mom never said anything about it in her last letter. As a matter of fact, she said none of the family would be using it. How did you manage to get away?"

"It was easy," he shrugged. "I took a page out of your book."

"What do you mean?" she frowned.

"I ran away," he stated, his expression not changing from its lazy grin.

"You what!" Shari was stunned by his answer. At times, Rory could be a terrible tease. She was half-convinced this was one of them.

"Close your mouth, Shari." He tapped the underside of her chin with his finger. "You're creating a draft." His glance wandered to her friends. "Granddad would be upset with your lack of manners, Sis. You haven't introduced me to your friends."

Prompted by his reminder, Shari went through the formality. "This is my younger brother, Rory Lancaster. These are two of my sorority sisters—Doré Evans and Beth Daniels."

"I'm Beth." She stepped forward to clarify the introduction. "Shari said it would be all right if we stayed here."

"It is as far as I'm concerned," Rory assured her. "We have an open-door policy in our family. Friends are always welcome."

"Is Mother coming?" Shari was visualizing all sorts of complications and trying to solve them before they occurred.

"No."

Something in his expression made Shari ask, "You were just joking earlier, weren't you?" She frowned because she suddenly wasn't sure. "You didn't leave Gold Leaf, did you?"

"I don't know why you have any doubts." His head moved to the side in an attitude of disappointment. "I thought you were the one person who would understand."

"But why? What happened?"

Rory was nineteen, two years her junior. He'd always seemed so carefree, never taking anything too seriously. She could never recall him arguing with anyone, certainly never his grandfather.

"You know what it's like at home," he reminded her. "With Mom always pushing me and Granddad pulling me, and Whit walking around as the shining example of what I should become, I couldn't take it any more."

Beth shifted uneasily and glanced at Doré. "Why don't we go upstairs and take our showers?" she suggested. "That way Shari and her brother can have some time alone."

In a position where she had to reluctantly agree or appear impolite, Doré still showed her desire to see the outcome of this unfolding drama.

"I suppose that would be the thing to do." She trailed slowly after Beth, lingering on the stairs to eavesdrop for as long as she could.

Shari eyed her younger brother with a grim sadness. "I didn't know you were having a difficult time at home."

"How could you?" Rory shrugged, but his glance contained a hint of condemnation. "You've hardly been home at all these last three years. You have your college, friends, and all sorts of activities. Sometimes I have the feeling you've forgotten all about us."

"That isn't true," she denied. "I don't come home very often because— You know why I don't so there isn't any point in going into my problems."

"Ever since you left, Granddad has been impossible to live with," he grumbled. "Between him and Mother, I've been practically smothered."

"Just because I rebelled against his authority, that didn't give him any right to take it out on you." She tried to control the rising temper that was invariably sparked by any discussion concerning the Lancaster patriarch. "You should have talked it over with Whit. Granddad listens to him."

"Whit doesn't know anything about it," Rory replied.

"Do you mean you haven't told him how you feel?" She studied her brother with confusion.

"He's busy. You know what it's like at this time of year." He attempted to justify his silence, then shrugged. "Besides I've never been able to talk to him about my problems. You have always been closer to him than I've been."

"That isn't true," she protested.

"Yes, it is. You've always confided everything in him," Rory insisted. "I remember how you used to slip into his bedroom at night. The two of you would talk for hours. Sometimes I'd lie in my bed listening to you and wish I could go in there."

"But why didn't you?" His revelation troubled her. They had never consciously excluded Rory from their late-night gatherings.

"I just didn't that's all." He shrugged his answer, revealing a regret that he'd even brought up the subject. "It doesn't matter."

Hesitating, Shari bit at the inside of her lip, then decided not to pursue the subject. "What are you going to do now?"

"I don't know yet," he admitted. "I'm just going to relax for a few days and think. But

I'm not cut out to be a tobacco farmer, Shari.'' His frustration surfaced in an impatient rush. "Heck, I can't even stand the smell of cigarette smoke!"

The remark sparked a childhood memory. "Do you remember that time we took a pack of Whit's cigarettes and sneaked into the garage to smoke them?'' A laughing smile spread across her features. "I was about ten years old and you were eight."

"Boy, do I remember!" he laughed. "It must have been a hundred and fifty degrees in that garage. It was stuffy, with no circulation. The smoke just hung there in a blue cloud around our heads."

"Every time we tried to inhale, we started coughing and choking," Shari recalled, laughing with him.

Looking back on the incident, she could see its humor. At the time, it had seemed like high adventure. There had been excitement in sneaking off to do something forbidden.

"You got sick afterward," she remembered and wondered if that had been the start of her younger brother's abhorrence of tobacco.

"I was never so sick in all my life!" Rory admitted. "And you just laughed."

"I'd never seen anybody turn green before," she defended her reaction of that long-ago time. "Mother was so worried about you."

"She never did guess what made me so sick." There was a lopsided grin slanting his mouth.

"Whit did, though."

"He did?" Rory expressed surprised. "He never said anything."

"No. He saw how sick you were and decided that we had been sufficiently punished for our little escapade," Shari replied.

"But how did he know?"

"I guess we reeked of tobacco smoke," she supposed. "He lectured me about being such a corrupting influence on you."

She remembered the glint that had been in Whit's eyes and realized now he had been amused by the results of their encounter with the demon tobacco. As she gazed at Rory, she saw that he was still following in her footsteps and her amusement faded.

"The family will probably find me guilty of leading you astray again, now that you've left home." Shari sighed.

"They shouldn't blame you. It's their own fault," he insisted.

"It can't be easy for them to accept, especially for Mother." She knew the furor her own leaving had caused. "I suppose there was a big scene.

"No." He shoved his hands deep into the pockets of his slacks and moved away, but not before Shari had glimpsed the vaguely guilty look on his face. Her gaze sharply narrowed in confusion.

"I can't believe that you left without them trying to stop you."

"I didn't tell them I was going." Before she could voice a reply, Rory turned to face her and justify his actions. "I told you that I took a page from your book. Whit was in the fields with the workers and Granddad was napping. Mom was at some ladies' club. I did the same thing you did—packed up and left when no one was around."

"Mother is going to be so upset." *Not to mention Granddad Lancaster,* Shari thought but only to herself. That didn't need to be said.

"I know. But I have my own life to live." He staunchly defended his right to do what he wanted, not what the family dictated.

"You did leave a note, didn't you?" Somehow she knew his answer.

"No."

"Oh, Rory." She shook her dark head in grim disapproval. "When you aren't there for dinner tonight, Mother is going to imagine all sorts of terrible things have happened to you. She'll be half out of her mind with worry. You'd better call and let them know where you are."

"I will," he promised, then qualified it. "—as soon as I know where I'm going and what I'm going to do. I need some time to think without anybody hassling me. So don't you start in on me, too, Shari."

The appeal for her support and understanding prompted Shari to swallow some of her anger for his inconsiderate behavior. "All right," she agreed tersely. "But I still think you are wrong for not letting Mother know where you are and assuring her that you are okay."

"Thanks, Shari." His mouth curved in a grateful smile. "I knew I could count on you to take my side in this."

What else could she do? Rory had placed her in the uncomfortable position of feeling responsible for his actions because he'd patterned them after her own. A rueful smile edged the corners of her mouth.

"Some vacation this is turning out to be," she murmured. "Instead of avoiding any squabbles with the Lancaster family, I find myself in the middle of one."

"I don't expect you to get involved in this," Rory stated. "No one has to know that you had any part in it. It was my decision, not yours."

"I know." But she hoped Granddad Lancaster saw it that way. They found enough subjects to argue about without adding Rory to the list.

"Since we have that settled, what are your plans for dinner tonight? Are you going out?" Rory returned to the subject related to his empty stomach.

"Yes. We came back to shower and change before going to the club," Shari explained.

"Is it all right if I come with you? I'm starved."

"Of course, you can." She didn't think Beth or Doré would object if he joined them.

"I guess I'd better shower and change, too." He walked toward his suitcase sitting at the foot of the stairs. "Is anybody using Whit's room?"

"No."

"In that case, I'll unpack my stuff in his room." Rory paused on the first step. "What time were you going to be ready to leave for dinner?"

"We'll meet you downstairs in about an hour," Shari replied.

"Okay," he agreed and turned to carry his suitcase up the stairs.

THE CLUBHOUSE was ideally situated to offer a view of both the eighteenth green of the golf course and the waters of Loch Dornie. Its beamed cathedral ceilings gave an Old World charm to the building. This theme was accented with furnishings from England and Scotland, the two countries that had made a lasting impression on the Appalachian Mountain chain.

Accompanied by Rory, the three girls were seated at a table near the dining room entrance. Shari absently fingered the cameo brooch attached to the black velvet choker around her neck. Her dress was made from white eyelet lace in an off-the-shoulder design. Its old-fashioned ambience seemed to be in keeping with the surroundings.

"Were you planning to go to the *Ceilidh* tonight?" Rory pronounced it as "kay-lee" as he addressed the question to the three girls in general and Shari in particular.

"I thought we might," she said, "if we finished dinner early enough."

"What is a *Ceilidh?*" Beth glanced from one to the other with a blank look.

"It's a get-together to play and sing old Scottish songs," Rory explained.

"I think I've had my fill of bagpipes for one day," Doré replied and showed her lack of appreciation for its unique music with a downward curve of distaste to her mouth.

"Don't pay any attention to Doré," Beth advised Rory. "She's bored by just about everything. You get used to it after a while."

"There is something that wouldn't bore me," Doré murmured with her gaze trained on the dining room entrance. "That man who just walked in."

Shari glanced over her shoulders to look at the man who had attracted such avid interest. There was something familiar about the tall, well-built man surveying the room to locate his party.

When he turned to face the direction of their table, her heart gave a glad leap of recognition. For a long second, his gaze was locked with hers. A suggestion of a smile touched his rugged, sunbronzed features as he started toward the table.

Rising to her feet, she didn't hear Rory's muffled curse. Her lips were parted in a silent laugh of delight, her green eyes sparkling as she glided forward to meet him. It seemed natural to walk right into his arms. Closing her eyes, she hugged him tight and rested her cheek against his smoothly shaven jaw.

"It seems so long since I've seen you, Whit," she declared with a sigh.

He smelled of tobacco and tangy aftershave, heady and familiar aromas that she always associated with him. His hands were around her waist, strong and firm in their pressure.

"It's only been since Easter," he mocked gently and brushed his mouth over her temple.

"Yes, but you were so busy that I hardly saw you at all except at the dinner table," she reminded him and returned the light caress of his mouth by pressing her lips firmly against his cheek.

Her red lipstick left a visible imprint of her kiss on his tanned skin. Shari laughed softly when she saw it and borrowed the handkerchief tucked in the breast pocket of his dark jacket.

"I've left my mark on you." She took her time wiping it off, peering at him through the upward sweep of her lashes and enjoying the golden warmth of his brown eyes as he watched her.

"You left your mark on me a long time ago." Whit took the handkerchief from her and stuffed it back into his pocket. His gaze swept her upturned face with an admiring, yet an aloof look. "It doesn't seem possible, but you seem to have grown more beautiful."

His lazy compliment sent a thrill of pleasure through her. "You are still the handsomest man I know," Shari countered.

She experienced a vague tingle of surprise as she realized her statement was the truth. She had yet to meet a man who could measure up to Whit in either looks or strength of character. Perhaps that was why she had never become seriously involved with anyone she'd dated.

When his hands applied pressure to set her away from him, she made an involuntary move of protest. She wasn't ready to end this warm reunion with her stepbrother. He arched an eyebrow in her direction, the glint of mockery in his look.

"People are going to get the impression I'm your long-lost lover if we don't break this up," Whit taunted in a low drawl.

It was the second time in a single day the word "lover" had been used in conjunction with him. A hot warmth spread across her face, reddening her cheeks as Shari pulled away from him. His eyes narrowed in sharpened interest on her face.

"Are you blushing, Shari?" he accused, a faint curve deepening the corners of his mouth.

"No," she denied that quickly and would have turned away from his penetrating gaze, but his hand caught her chin and forced her to stay where she was.

"Yes, you are," he insisted lazily. "Does it embarrass you to think of me as a lover?"

She was reluctantly conscious of the pressure of his strong fingers against her cheek and throat. There was a sensation of intimacy in their touch that she couldn't explain. Her pulse began hammering in her throat. Shari recoiled from the possibility that this disturbance was caused by any physical attraction.

A mask settled over his features, blocking out his thoughts. His hand came away from her chin, letting her go as he appeared to lose interest in her answer.

"Never mind," Whit said. "You don't need to answer that. It was a foolish question." He offered her his arm. "Shall we join the others at the table?"

As she turned and slipped her hand inside the crook of his arm, she questioned the reason for his unexpected appearance. "What brought you here?" Her gaze wandered to the table where it rested on Rory's grim expression. She immediately knew the answer to her question. "You came because of Rory, didn't you?"

Whit slanted her a downward glance that seemed silently alert. "Yes." It was a simple, straightforward answer that told her nothing of his intentions or his reaction to Rory's flight from home.

They had reached the table and it was impossible for Shari to find out where his sympathies rested before he confronted Rory. Whit was too intelligent not to have guessed Rory had been influenced indirectly by her. Yet he hadn't seemed upset or angry with her so perhaps he could be won over to Rory's side.

Those questions and their answers would have to wait until later. Doré was waiting expectantly for an introduction, prodding Shari with a hard look. That impatience was completely absent when Doré turned her gaze on Whit. The gleam in her blue eyes was subtly provocative.

Dislike rushed through Shari at how obvious the blonde was acting. Her hand tightened fractionally on his arm as Shari briskly made the introductions.

"It is a pleasure to meet you at last, Mr. Lancaster," Doré purred and held out her long-nailed hand, forcing Whit to take it in greeting. "Shari has told us so much about you."

"Oh?" He arched another look at Shari, one that questioned and taunted. "Too bad I wasn't a mouse in a corner. It might have been very enlightening to discover what she said about me."

The warmth was again in her cheeks as Shari recalled the conversation. The fact didn't escape Whit's notice. Doré didn't like the way Whit had become distracted by her remark and quickly set about to correct the situation.

"Yes, Shari thinks you are the best brother any girl could have," she lightly stressed the family relationship.

Whit smiled as he released Doré's hand. "That's quite a compliment." There was something distant about the second glance he gave Shari. "I hope I can always live up to your expectations."

"Have you had dinner, Mr. Lancaster?" Beth inquired.

"No, I haven't," he admitted, then corrected her. "I would like it if you would call me Whit."

"Why don't you join us for dinner, Whit?" Doré invited, quick to dispense with the formal address. "I'm sure the waiter can find us a table that will seat five."

"Do you mind?" Whit put the question to Shari, his tone soft and inquiring.

"Of course not." Although she guessed that Rory wasn't too keen about the idea.

Despite the fact that the dining room was crowded, their waiter succeeded in seating them at a larger table after only a slight delay. Shari was irritated when she realized that Doré had maneuvered it so Whit was sitting beside her. It was also apparent that her friend intended to monopolize his attention.

"I understand you own a tobacco plantation, Whit." Doré leaned toward him. "What's it like? I confess I know absolutely nothing about it."

"It's like any other crop. You plant it, harvest it and sell it." He summed it up with a minimum of words.

Shari bent her head to conceal an amused smile. Whit was not like other men. That old technique of getting a man to talk about himself would not work with him. He had seen through Doré's ploy just as she had done. Shari was silently glad and wondered if she wasn't being disloyal to her college classmate.

"You must admit that there is a great deal of romance attached to tobacco plantations, Whit," Doré insisted, not deterred from the subject.

"I think that depends on your viewpoint," he replied and leveled a glance at his half brother. "Don't you, Rory?"

Rory pressed his lips together in a thin line. He hadn't said a word since Whit had arrived. His stiff silence came to an end as he broached the reason Whit had come.

"If you came all this way to make me go back with you, you might as well forget it. I'm not going back," he challenged.

"I don't think this is the place to discuss it, Rory," Whit quietly censured him.

"How did you know I was here anyway?" Rory challenged.

"Where else would you go?" Whit reasoned. "You had to have a place to sleep. It was logical for you to come here."

"You just made a wild guess and got lucky." Rory refused to believe it had been anything else.

"You could say that," Whit conceded and cast a sideways glance at Shari. "I have to admit that I didn't expect to find Shari here. Your mother is under the impression that you're staying with friends at Cape Hatteras."

"I never told her that," Shari denied his insinuation that she had deliberately lied to her mother.

"But you let her believe that," Whit guessed. "I suppose you arranged to meet Rory here to give him moral support."

"No, I didn't. I had no idea of his plans until he showed up here this afternoon." She was hurt that Whit believed she had conspired with Rory to run away from home.

"That's the truth, Whit," Rory supported her statement. "I didn't know she was here." He paused, a look of concern flickering across his expression. "I hope Mom wasn't too upset when she realized I'd left."

"I find it hard to believe that you care what your mother felt." His look was harsh, revealing the unrelenting side of his nature.

"I do so care!" Rory reacted vigorously to the denunciation.

"Then why didn't you have the courage to tell her your plans?" Whit challenged. "If you couldn't face her, the least you could have done was to leave her a note so she wouldn't worry herself half-sick."

"I—" Rory faltered under the silently piercing attack. "I wanted to decide where I was going and what I wanted to do first. I was going to call her in a couple of days."

"You're going to call her as soon as we've had dinner." It was an order. It couldn't be mistaken for anything else.

"But what am I going to tell her?" Rory argued. "She's going to ask me questions that I can't answer yet."

"You could just tell her that you're going to spend a couple of days here," Shari suggested. "Until you make up your mind about what you're going to do next, you can let her think you're just here for a long weekend."

"I suppose I could," he replied hesitantly. "What do you think, Whit?"

"It's the same thing I told her before I left."

"Do you mean . . . you gave me an alibi?" Rory was stunned.

"I had to tell Elizabeth something to ease her mind," Whit said, referring to their mother by her given name.

"Gee, thanks, Whit. I don't know what to say." He shook his head in astonishment.

"You can thank me by phoning your mother and reassuring her that you are all right." The stern line of his mouth relaxed into a faint curve. Then Whit noticed the waiter hovering near the table and opened his menu. "Has everyone decided what they would like to order for dinner?"

CHAPTER THREE

AFTER DINNER, they all returned to the condominium. Doré had volunteered to ride back with Whit in his car and Shari had been forced to stifle her irritation again at the sight of the two of them together. She was troubled by her sudden desire to compete for Whit's attention, and her possessive attitude toward her stepbrother.

"This is the perfect night for a moonlight sail," Doré declared as they walked to the apartment door. "There's a good breeze and the moon is full. Didn't you mention at dinner that you kept a boat here, Whit?"

"Yes, I do," he admitted and moved smoothly ahead of Shari to unlock the door.

Since he had ignored her broad hint, Doré made her desire plainer. "Why don't we all go for a sail tonight?" But she looked only at Whit when she made her suggestion.

Shari gritted her teeth at her friend's boldness and silently studied Whit's expression as he opened the door to admit them. There was nothing in his rugged features to indicate he regarded Doré as being too forward. If anything, he appeared vaguely indulgent. He waited until everyone was inside before he responded to her suggestion.

"You and Beth are welcome to use the sailboat tonight. This is your vacation and I don't wish to interfere with your enjoyment of it, but I'm afraid that we—" His glance swept over Rory and Shari to define the pronoun. "—have a family matter to settle. Would you excuse us?"

"Of course." Doré tried not to show her displeasure with his decision but she didn't succeed too well.

Whit half-turned to throw a look at Rory. "We'll use the telephone in the study to call your mother."

With obvious reluctance, Rory crossed the beige carpet to the study door and Shari followed him a step ahead of Whit. Referring to the room as a study seemed almost inappropriate. It was a bright and airy room with hanging greenery. The cranberry-upholstered sofa made a splash of color against white walls. When the door was closed, Rory hesitated and glanced uncertainly at Whit.

"You know the number." Whit motioned toward the telephone sitting on an oak table and crossed the room to the sliding glass doors. He opened them and stepped outside to light a cigarette while Rory picked up the telephone to dial the number.

Shari wandered over to the doors and leaned against the frame. Her gaze was drawn to Whit's profile, sharply etched by the moonlight. It was a compelling face, lean and strong, roughly masculine. His brown hair glinted with gold lights, stirred by the night's breeze.

Behind her, she was absently aware of Rory speaking to her mother on the telephone, but she was consciously noticing Whit's hard muscled frame. It unnerved her to discover that her senses were tuning in to his latent sexuality. When his roaming glance touched her, she had to look away before he saw the awareness in her eyes.

"Shari," Rory cupped his hand over the mouthpiece of the receiver as he urgently whispered her name.

Seeing the concern written in his expression, she pushed away from the door frame to walk quickly to him. "What is it?" She kept her voice low, not wanting to make her presence known to the woman on the other end of the line.

"It's Mom," he said. "She's worried about you now. When I disappeared this afternoon, she tried to get in touch with you. When you weren't with that family on the Coast, she—" He left the rest to her imagination. "Shari, she's frantic." He was half-listening to the anxious voice on the other end of the line. "She wants to know if I know where you are. What should I tell her?"

"You might as well talk to her," Whit said. She pivoted when his voice came from directly behind her. She hadn't been aware he had followed her inside. He eyed her steadily. "Elizabeth won't be satisfied until she hears your voice."

He was right. She sighed a grudging admission and nodded to Rory that she would talk to her. Nothing had gone right since her vacation had started. Deceptions were bound to become unraveled sooner or later, she realized.

Rory handed her the phone. "Hello, Mother?" she said with forced brightness.

At first there was silence on the other end of the line. Then an uncertain female voice came back to question, "Shari? Is that you?"

"Yes, Mother. I'm sorry if I worried you, but I'm fine," she assured her.

"But what are you doing there? I thought you were going to stay with Judge Fullmore and his daughter at Nag's Head. When I called them and they said you weren't there—"

Shari interrupted her. "They invited me but I had already made plans to spend my vacation time with Beth Daniels and Doré Evans, two girls who belong to my sorority. I must not have explained it very well in my letter to you. I'm sorry for causing you concern, Mother," she apologized.

"As long as you are all right, I guess that's all that matters." Her mother sounded confused and uncertain. "But I'm sure you didn't mention you were going to be at Grandfather Mountain."

"They're holding the Highland Games this weekend," Shari reminded her. "Neither Beth or Doré had ever seen them. When you wrote in your letter that you wouldn't be using the condominium this summer, it seemed an opportune time to come here.''

"Yes, of course," she agreed absently. ''Then you will be coming home for a few days on your vacation?''

"I don't know for sure," she hedged against committing herself.

"But you are so close," her mother protested.

"I know. It's just that . . . my friends have made other plans." It was a weak excuse. Even Shari heard its false ring.

"Shari, are you sure everything is all right?" her mother questioned. "Is there something you aren't telling me?"

"No, of course not." She answered the last question first. "I'm fine, Mother, really."

Her reply was followed by several seconds of silence before Elizabeth Lancaster spoke again. "Is Whit there?"

"Yes," she assured her in the event she thought he had come to some harm.

"May I speak to him?" her mother requested.

"Yes. Just a minute." Turning to Whit, she handed him the phone. "She wants to talk to you now," she said and shrugged her ignorance of the reason.

When he took the receiver from her, Shari moved away. Rory was standing to one side, wearing a dispirited expression. She walked over to him.

"How did it go?" she asked gently.

"I hate being the baby of the family," he muttered in a spate of self-pity. "Nobody lets you grow up. I'm nineteen but the way Mom acts, you'd think I was nine."

Her gaze strayed back to Whit, but his one-word answers didn't enlighten her as to the reason her mother wanted to speak to him. She returned her attention to her younger half brother.

"You're right. Mother will probably still treat you the same way when you're twenty-nine," she sympathized.

"How am I ever going to be able to convince her that I can take care of myself?" Rory wanted to know.

"You won't."

"Boy, you are real encouraging!" He flashed her an irritated look. "If you want to be helpful, I could use some suggestions on how I'm going to convince Mother that I want to leave. I don't want to hurt her but I feel trapped at Gold Leaf. Whit thrives on all that pressure, but I can't take it.''

Whit was off the phone and had joined them in time to hear the last of Rory's protests. ''What is it that you want, Rory?'' he asked.

''That's just it! I don't know.'' He revealed his inner frustration. ''All I know is what I don't want.''

''Give yourself time,'' Whit consoled patiently. ''You're young yet.''

Rory glared at him, then shifted his glance to Shari. ''Do you see what I mean?'' he accused. ''Nobody thinks I'm grown up!'' He stalked from the room.

Whit darted Shari an amused glance. ''I have the feeling I said the wrong thing.''

''That's an understatement.'' She smiled as Whit moved away to settle into the matching armchair to the cranberry-colored sofa. She watched him light another cigarette and return the lighter to his pocket. ''He was just complaining about being the 'baby' of the family. He's convinced that no one thinks he's old enough to make his own decisions.''

"Which is why he is so angry with himself because he doesn't know what he wants." Whit concluded with a throaty chuckle. "It must be hell."

"It is." Her smile broadened. Then she remembered. "Why did Mother want to talk to you?"

The glitter of amusement in his eyes grew brighter. "She wanted to ask if I had met your 'friends.'"

His answer and his expression confused her. "Why?"

"You sounded so reluctant to bring them to Gold Leaf that Elizabeth became suspicious," Whit replied.

"Suspicious? Of what?" Shari was more confused.

"She thought you might be vacationing in 'mixed' company; that some of your 'friends' might be men," he explained with dry insinuation.

"Do you mean that she thought that I—" Shari couldn't finish the sentence.

"Yes. It occurred to her that you might be 'sleeping' with one of your male friends and since you knew how strongly Granddad would disapprove of such an arrangement, you didn't want to bring them home," he said it for her.

"Why would she think something like that?" she demanded on an incredulous note.

"I imagine she has been listening to her lady friends recounting stories about wild college girls and started worrying about her little girl." Whit tapped his cigarette in the ashtray. "You have had three years exposure to college life—without parental supervision or guidance. It's natural for her to wonder if you'd had an affair with a man—or are having one."

"Well, I'm not and I haven't!" Shari denied that allegation vigorously. "How could she think that about me?"

"You have never made it any secret that you date frequently," he reasoned.

"That doesn't mean I go to bed with them," she retorted.

"I wasn't suggesting that she thought you were promiscuous," Whit replied calmly. "But it is reasonable to assume you could have been attracted to one of your dates."

"I have been attracted to several men but none to that extent!" Shari insisted.

"You are a beautiful woman. And I seriously doubt that you are frigid." He was watching her closely. "I never would have guessed that you were so hard to please."

"I guess I am!" She felt her anger growing at the way he was cross-examining her. "If I'm too particular, then it's all your fault!"

"Mine?" He raised an eyebrow at that.

"Yes, yours!" She moved toward his chair to emphasize her point.

His gaze narrowed. "Why is it mine?"

"Because—" She suddenly realized how heated the exchange had become.

The last thing she wanted to do was argue with him. She paused, releasing the tension that had built inside with a short laugh and sat down on the arm of his chair.

"Because nobody measures up to you." She gazed at him with a certain pride and curved a hand behind his neck, letting it rest on the sinewed cords running from his neck to his shoulder. Her fingers absently rubbed them. "I haven't met a man yet who has all that my brother does. I guess I'm just not prepared to settle for less."

Instead of appearing pleased by her compliment, his expression became hard. "Don't put me on a pedestal, Shari,'' he warned. ''I don't belong there.''

''Can I help it if I want a man like my stepbrother?'' She tried to tease him into smiling. When that failed, she bent to lightly kiss his cheek.

Whit abruptly stood up, nearly unbalancing Shari from her perch on the chair's arm. ''You expect too much from me.''

His attitude puzzled her and she frowned. ''I don't understand.''

He breathed in deeply and released it, a weary resignation stealing over his expression. ''Yes, that's the problem,'' he said cryptically, and reached in his shirt pocket for another cigarette. ''Your friends are waiting for you.''

''You aren't making any sense.'' She shook her head, unable to fathom his meaning.

''Probably not,'' Whit agreed and snapped the lighter flame to the tip of his cigarette. ''I've had a lot on my mind lately.''

It seemed a reasonable explanation, one that Shari was willing to accept. ''And Rory and I aren't helping matters any, are we?'' she realized. ''I'm sure you had more important things to do this weekend than come traipsing up here.''

"I had other things to do but not necessarily more important things,'' he corrected. "Now, scram! Give a guy a chance to smoke his cigarette in peace.''

"Yes, sir!'' She laughed, relieved to see his mood change and turned away to leave the room.

"Would you bring me the extra blankets?'' Whit requested. "It's too late to be playing musical chairs with the upstairs bedrooms. Everyone's all unpacked and settled in, so we might as well leave the sleeping arrangements as they stand.''

"Oh, but—'' Shari turned to protest.

His dark eyes were squinted at the smoke from the cigarette dangling out of the corner of his mouth as he worked the knot of his tie loose and stripped it off.

"This sofa folds out into a bed. I'll sleep here tonight,'' he stated.

Shari hesitated, aware of the logic of his decision yet feeling there was a more comfortable solution. "If you insist,'' she replied finally.

"I insist." Whit smiled at her with his eyes, a spray of lines radiating from the corners. "Go get the blankets."

"I'll bring them right back," she promised and walked out of the study, closing the door behind her.

The extra bedding was kept in the linen closet in the upstairs hall. Shari ran up the steps to fetch it and take it back to Whit. When she reached the top of the stairs, Beth was just coming out of Doré's room.

"We've decided to accept Whit's offer to use his boat and go for a midnight sail," Beth told her. "Rory is coming, too. He's in his room changing. Do you want to go with us?"

"Yes, but first—" She walked to the linen closet and opened the door to collect the extra blankets and pillows, "—I have to take this down to Whit."

"Don't bother to hurry," Beth advised and gestured toward the room Doré was using. "Doré hasn't made up her mind what she's going to wear yet. You have plenty of time."

Shari laughed, aware that their friend had a notorious reputation about the length of time it took her to dress. Of course, the end result was usually perfection, too, so perhaps the time was justified. While Beth continued to her own room, Shari carried the bedding down the stairs to the study. She knocked once and walked in.

In her absence, Whit had removed his suit jacket as well as his tie. His white dress shirt was unbuttoned at the throat and the sleeves were rolled up, revealing the dark tan of his forearms.

He was seated behind the oak worktable with his briefcase opened on its top and a stack of papers spread in front of him. He glanced up when she entered the room, a pre-occupied look to his expression.

"I don't suppose there is ever an end to paper work," Shari observed with a sympathetic glance at the briefcase brimming with notes and reports.

"It's self-perpetuating," Whit agreed and pushed his chair back from the table to stand.

"It will only take a minute to make your bed." She set the blankets on the cushion of the armchair and began removing the throw pillows and seat cushions from the sofa. "I didn't mean to disturb you."

"You always do, so why should this time be any different." There was a wry slant to his mouth as he walked around the table to the sofa.

"When have I ever bothered you when you were working?" Shari challenged, ready to argue the point because she knew she was always careful not to interrupt him when he was busy.

"All the time." The glint in his eyes told Shari that she was being baited even if the rest of his expression appeared dead serious. "I'll help you lift the hide-a-bed out."

Shari stepped to one side so Whit could fold out the mattress, assured now of his true reason for pausing in his paper work. The sofa bed was sometimes stubborn and required a little manhandling to lie out straight. She watched the muscles in his shoulders and arms flex and ripple under the shirt as he pulled the hide-a-bed out and folded it out flat. She had always known he was strong, but she had never thought of him in terms of hard flesh and bone.

For the span of a second, her wayward imagination tried to recall what he looked like in brief swimming trunks. Shari blocked out the picture before the image became clear, appalled by her sudden interest in his body.

Turning away, she picked up the bottom sheet and shook it out to fall across the mattress. Whit moved out of her way while she tucked the sides under. She could feel his eyes watching her as she made the bed. By the time she was through except for the pillows, Shari began having second thoughts about Whit sleeping on the lumpy bed.

As she tucked the pillow under her chin to slip it into its case, she suggested a trade of sleeping quarters. "You don't have to stay here, Whit. You can sleep in my bed."

"With you?" His tone was lightly suggestive.

She stopped shaking the pillow into its case and turned to face him. First, there had been the comment that she disturbed him—now he was deliberately insinuating that her offer had been that they should sleep together.

Had he always said things like that? Or had she just become sensitive to the double meanings in his remarks because of her newfound awareness of him?

Whit studied her faintly openmouthed look and smiled lazily. "No thanks, Shari. I remember how loud you snore."

He was teasing her again she realized and her tension dissipated with the faded concern. "Whit Lancaster, I do not snore! How could you say such a thing!" She hit him with the pillow and laughed.

"You snore louder than a buzz saw," he accused with a throaty laugh and grabbed at the pillow to wrench it from her grasp. "I've heard you."

"It was probably you snoring!" Shari retorted as they fought over the pillow. "I don't make a sound when I sleep."

The years faded away and this became another version of one of their many pillow fights. Laughing, they tussled over the pillow. Shari lost her balance and fell backward onto the bed with a gasping shriek of laughter, pulling Whit onto the mattress with her. She lost her grip on the pillow as they rolled together on the bed, and ceased trying to reclaim it.

"I give up. You win." She breathlessly declared him the victor and paused to rest from her struggle.

His arm remained under her back as he positioned the pillow so both of them could lay their heads on it. "That's where it belongs anyway," he stated.

Lying side by side on their backs, they gazed at the ceiling. Shari hadn't felt this close to him in a long time. She turned her cheek against the pillow to look at him. His roughly virile features seemed to be chiseled out of sun-warmed teakwood. She wished this moment could last forever but she knew it was impossible.

"I suppose you have to drive home first thing in the morning," she sighed.

"No."

Her jade-green eyes widened in faint surprise. "How long are you staying then?"

Whit turned his head on the pillow to face her. "I plan to stay until Rory makes up his mind what he's going to do—unless he takes too long about it."

She watched his mouth forming the words and became fascinated by its masculine shape. It was firm, and clearly drawn. There was nothing soft or weak about it. A dark, forbidden longing rose in her to feel his strong lips against her own. Her heart started knocking against her ribs with unusual force, awakening Shari to the direction her thoughts were taking. Not trusting herself so close to him, she sat up and smoothed the eyelet material of her skirt.

"Beth and the others are waiting for me," Shari explained away her sudden movement. Her backward glance saw that Whit had raised himself on one elbow, his narrowed look creating a frown. "We're going to take you up on your offer to use the boat and go for a moonlight sail. I shall have to change clothes." As she stood up on one side of the bed, Whit was straightening to his feet on the other. "I suppose you'll finish the paper work you brought with you."

"Yes. That's unfortunately the only way it will get done." His smile was pleasant, yet Shari detected an air of reserve about him. "Enjoy yourself."

"We will." Quick, gliding strides carried her to the door.

Her smile was artificially bright to hide her inner uncertainty. As she left the study, Rory, Beth and Doré were coming down the stairs, dressed for sailing. She started up the steps, meeting them at a point short of halfway.

"What was going on down here?" Doré demanded, sweeping Shari with an accusing look. "You certainly were making enough noise in there with Whit. We could hear you laughing all the way upstairs."

While Shari hesitated over an answer, Rory supplied the explanation. "That's not unusual. Those two have always carried on like that."

Shari didn't elaborate on the response. "It shouldn't take me more than a couple of minutes to change, then I'll be right down." Beth moved to the side so Shari could pass and continue up the stairs to her room.

In all, it took Shari a little less than ten minutes to change out of her dress into a pair of navy blue twill slacks, a pale blue turtleneck and white sneakers. On top of the outfit, she added a dark blue windbreaker and tied a scarf of blue-green silk around her black hair.

She half-ran down the stairs to join the sailing party waiting for her. It wasn't until she was nearly to the bottom that Shari noticed they didn't seem to be in any hurry—at least Doré wasn't.

Whit was in the living room with them, acting the polite host by keeping them company in her absence. Doré had sidled close to him to subtly and aggressively flirt with him, and Whit didn't seem to object.

A hot knife of jealousy stabbed Shari. She walked forward, determined to break up the scene. "Why is everybody standing around?" she challenged, deliberately ignoring the fact that they had been waiting for her. "Let's go."

Rory and Beth were quite willing to be hurried along but Doré lingered next to Whit. "Change your mind and come with us, Whit," she coaxed with a sexy smile. "You'll miss out on a lot of fun."

The lazily indulgent way he was regarding her blonde sorority sister made Shari feel raw. When he didn't immediately turn down the invitation, she stepped in to do it for him.

"Whit can't come. He has work to do," she stated in a very emphatic voice.

There was a glint of mocking humor in his eyes when he swung his glance to her, amused that she had found it necessary to remind him of it. She was immediately irritated with herself for speaking out.

Whit turned back to Doré. "I'm afraid Shari is right. I have a lot of paper work I need to finish."

"Well, if I can't persuade you—" Doré sighed her disappointment and didn't bother to finish the sentence, lifting her shoulders in a little shrug to indicate her reluctant acceptance of his decision.

Then Whit was directing his glance at Shari and Rory, once again assuming the role of older brother. "Be careful."

"We will," Rory promised and turned to the others. "Shall we go?"

There was a general exodus toward the door.

CHAPTER FOUR

IT WAS a perfect night for sailing. The moon was fat and full, gilding the waters of Loch Dornie with its silvery light. A stiff breeze filled the canvas to send the sailboat gliding silently through the water while the shadowed darkness of Grandfather Mountain watched over them.

But Shari wasn't in the mood to enjoy it. There were too many disquieting thoughts going around in her head. They left little room to consider the serenity of the moonlight sail. After an hour's ride, Rory maneuvered the boat into its slip to tie it up. Shari was glad it was over so she no longer had to maintain the pretense that she was having a good time.

On the way back to the condominium, Doré, Beth and Rory talked so much that her silence went unnoticed. It was much too early to consider sleep, plus the night sail had invigorated all of them, including Shari, although the others were more boisterous.

"Let's fix some hot toddies," Doré suggested as they entered the condo.

"Sorry," Rory tipped his head to the side in a gesture of regret. "Granddad never leaves any liquor here. He brings his private stock with him whenever we come."

"Hot chocolate is about the best we can do." Shari backed up his assertion. "I saw some cocoa in the cupboard."

"Didn't I see some peppermint canes in a candy jar?" Beth frowned as she tried to recall. "We can use them as swizzle sticks. They add a delicious minty flavor to hot cocoa."

"It sounds a little more exotic than plain cocoa," Doré commented and indicated how tame she considered the innocuous drink to be.

"Shall we fix some?" Beth directed her question to Shari.

But it was Doré who responded. "Yes, why don't you," she urged the two of them. "And I'll see if Whit would like a cup."

Shari was closer to the closed door of the study than Doré. She took advantage of the fact. "I'll ask him." She moved quickly toward the study, that possessive streak rearing its head again. "Rory can show you where everything is in the kitchen."

Unable to reach the door ahead of Shari, Doré was forced to accept the situation or get into a demeaning battle over Whit. It was not her nature to openly do battle over a man so the disgruntled blonde followed Beth and Rory to the kitchen.

Shari lightly rapped twice on the door but there was no response. She hesitated, then turned the knob, opening the door a crack to peer inside. A lamp burned at the desk where Whit was hunched over some papers. The artificial light caught the sheen of sun-streaks in his dark hair.

With the ease of long familiarity, she rested her hands on the corded shoulder muscles at the base of his neck, feeling their knotted tension. Whit stiffened at her initial touch, then it eased away when she began to gently knead the taut muscles. He leaned against the chair back, laying down his pen.

His right hand reached up to cover hers and press it firmly with affection before his fingers glided up to circle her wrist and draw her around to the side of his chair where he could see her. The suggestion of tiredness seemed to leave his features when a small curve lifted the corners of his mouth in a faint smile.

"I see you made it back from your moonlight sail." The pressure of his grip pulled her down to sit on the wooden armrest of the chair. "Nobody fell overboard? Nobody was hurt?"

Shari smiled at his teasing questions. "We had a marvelous time, completely without mishap," she assured him.

"That must be a record." Dryness rustled his voice.

His hand continued to hold her forearm at the wrist. Its light touch was making her pulse act up and Shari wondered if he could feel its erratic beat. She wasn't comfortable with this new sensual awareness of his male attraction.

"We're fixing some hot chocolate and wondered if you would like to take a break and have a cup with us," she explained her reason for coming to see him.

"You're actually inviting me to join you?" Despite his mocking tone, the slight drawl in his voice was infinitely pleasing to her ear. "Earlier I had the impression you wanted to keep my nose to the grindstone."

It was a direct reference to her insistence that he couldn't come sailing with them because he had work to do. Shari was well aware of her reasons for saying that then, but she had no intention of telling him what they were. She changed the subject instead.

"I don't know how you find time to do all that you do," she said because she was only beginning to realize the vital role he played in all their lives. "Our family would fall apart if it wasn't for you. You hold all of us together. Mother would worry herself sick if you weren't there to reassure her. You keep Granddad pacified. You're so patient with Rory. And any time I've ever needed you, you've been there. On top of that, you run the farm and take care of all the business. Why do you do it, Whit?" Shari wouldn't have blamed him if he had told them all to take a running jump into some lake.

"Because you matter to me," he answered without hesitation, regarding her steadily. A quiver of disturbance ran through her at his statement. Shari caught the flash of impatience in his gaze before it swung away from her and he let go of her arm. "Family is important, Shari."

"Yes, of course," she agreed, but she couldn't shake the strange feeling that she hadn't understood what he meant. She slipped off the armrest to stand beside the chair. "Will you have a cup of hot chocolate with us?" Shari repeated her earlier question.

Whit sliced her a look that was hard. "When have I ever told you 'no'? You've always had your own way." She was puzzled by his attitude and his challenge. In the next second, he made a complete reversal, a smile wiping out the austere lines to charm her. "Let's go have that hot chocolate."

As they left the study to join the others in the kitchen, Shari was plagued by a bewildering array of questions. Were his remarks double-edged or was she imagining it? Had he always looked at her like that or was she reading something into his looks that didn't exist? Had his attitude toward her changed or was she just now noticing it? And was it natural to feel so possessive toward him in the face of Doré's pursuit?

It was the latter Shari had to struggle to subdue when they entered the kitchen and Doré went to work on him. Whit was friendly and polite to her, neither encouraging nor discouraging her interest. Shari was barely able to taste the peppermint-flavored hot chocolate, too conscious of the way her beautiful sorority sister was monopolizing Whit.

Within minutes after he'd finished his cocoa, Whit made his apologies and returned to the study to finish his paper work. The minute the four of them were alone, Doré turned on her.

"What is the matter with you, Shari?" she demanded.

"With me?" She looked at her friend in surprise. "There's nothing wrong with me. What makes you think there is?"

"I wish you could see the way you've been acting and you wouldn't ask the question," Doré retorted in a huff.

"The way *I've* been acting?" Shari flared at the implication that her behavior had been questionable. "You're the one who's been drooling all over Whit, making an absolute fool of yourself."

"I didn't notice that he objected," she countered with an airy toss of her head.

"Whit has been raised to have better manners than that," Shari informed her snappishly.

"Obviously you weren't," Doré accused. "You've been throwing daggers at me since you came into the kitchen."

"Don't be ridiculous," Shari scoffed in an attempted denial of the charge.

"I'm not," she insisted. "If you have a prior claim on Whit, I wish you'd say so instead of pretending you only regard him as your older brother."

"That's what he is." Her assertion came quickly, perhaps too quickly. She was pricked by a feeling of unease with her answer and sought to defend her behavior. "I don't want Whit getting the wrong impression about my friends. That's all."

"I can tell he thinks a lot of you," Beth assured her, seeking to mend the rift between Shari and Doré. "I wouldn't worry about him thinking badly of you because of the actions of a friend."

"I suppose you're against me, too," Doré accused Beth.

"It's your nature to be forward." Beth was the stabilizing influence on the volatile per-

sonalities of her two friends. "I don't con-
demn you for it, and I'm positive Shari
doesn't either. It's only natural for a person to
want their family to like their choice of
friends."

"I don't know what you're squabbling
among yourselves about," Rory inserted.
"Whit is going to make up his own mind regardless of what anybody else thinks about
someone. He always does." The topic no
longer interested him. "Is there any more hot
chocolate left?"

"About half a cup, I think," Beth replied.

"I might as well drink it," he decided.
"There's no sense pouring it down the drain."

Although the disagreement was shelved,
they weren't able to regain the sociable mood.
When the cups and pan were washed, they
gravitated toward the upstairs bedrooms. A
light shone through the crack at the base of
the study door as the four climbed the stairs.

Sleep eluded Shari for a long time after she
crawled into bed. She tossed and turned, trying to sort through the confusion of her
changing attitude toward Whit. It was late
when she finally dozed off.

The strident ring of the doorbell interrupted her sleep, its penetrating summons prodding her into a semiwakefulness. She dragged herself out of bed and grabbed for the robe lying at the foot, pulling it around her as she hurried to the stairs.

At the same instant that she flipped on the switch to light the stairs, a light went on in the living room. The sudden brightness hurt her eyes and Shari had to pause and turn her head away, partially closing her eyes until they could adjust to the influx of light.

The doorbell rang loudly again and she descended one more step to answer it when she saw Whit crossing the living room from the study. He was clad only in the slacks he'd been wearing earlier that night; the upper half of his body was naked.

She couldn't help noticing how well-muscled he was, compact and firm, covered by tanned flesh. In her present state, just awakening from sleep, Shari had no immunity from such a blatant example of his maleness.

Some small sound must have betrayed her presence, because he glanced over his shoulder and saw her poised on the staircase. His recognition prompted her into action, over-riding the desire to stare at him.

"What time is it?" Her voice still held some of sleep's thickness as she continued down the steps.

"A little before three," he answered with similar huskiness. "Go back to your room. I'll see who's at the door."

Shari didn't listen to his suggestion. "But who could it be at this hour?"

"It's probably someone in the wrong building." Whit walked to the door.

The security chain was in place as he un-locked the dead bolt to open the door part way. Shari hovered in the middle of the living room. She had no intention of going to her room until she found out who it was. Whit's tall frame blocked the small opening, pre-venting her from seeing the person or per-sons standing outside.

"May I help you?" Something in the sharpness of Whit's tone alerted Shari that his initial guess had been wrong.

"Are you Whit Lancaster?" A clipped, male voice inquired.

"Yes, I am," he admitted.

"We're State Patrol officers. May we speak to you a minute?" came the request.

There was a slight pause and Shari guessed that they were showing Whit their identification. Little fingers of alarm were shooting through her as she tried to guess the portent of their presence. When Whit opened the door and the two uniformed officers stepped inside, she moved forward, searching their expressions.

"What is it?" she asked. "What's happened?"

"We've been asked to notify you of a family emergency," the first officer explained to Whit and glanced uncertainly at Shari. "The young lady—"

"—is my stepsister, Shari Sutherland," Whit identified her as she came to stand beside him.

"A family emergency?" She repeated the phrase in a frozen voice. "Is it Granddad?"

"Your brother is here as well?" the second officer asked Whit.

"Yes," Whit nodded. "What is the nature of the emergency?"

"It's a medical emergency. Mr. Frederick Lancaster asked us to contact you since he

couldn't reach you by phone," the first officer explained.

"But it's working," Shari insisted. "We
used it earlier tonight to call home."

"I'm sorry, Miss, but the telephone company informed us that an automobile acci-
dent has temporarily put this area out of
service. They expect the lines to be repaired by
morning." The first officer, and the older of
the two, didn't dispute her claim, and turned
back to Whit. "Mr. Lancaster asked you to
come home as quickly as you could."

"But—what's happened?" Shari asked
with a growing sense of panic. She clutched at
Whit's arm, needing the steadiness of his
strength to support her. "Who—"

"I don't wish to be the one to bring bad
news." Despite the phrases indicating apology, there was a certain bluntness to his
speech. "Your mother has suffered a stroke
and has been rushed to the hospital. Her condition is serious."

Her knees buckled in shock as she reeled
from the announcement that hit her like a
physical blow. Whit quickly gathered her
shaky body into his arms, holding her close.

Her head moved from side to side in numbed disbelief.

"No," she murmured. "It can't be."

"Would you get word to my grandfather that we'll be leaving directly?" Whit asked the patrolmen over the top of her bent head.

"Of course."

She was too stunned by the news to hear the men leave and the door close. Her blood was running cold. Not even the heat generated by Whit's body could warm her, although his strong arms held her so close she was practically enveloped in them. There were tears in her eyes when Shari lifted her head to look at him.

"It can't be true." She didn't want to believe it, but his grim expression convinced her. "Not Mother."

"Yes. At her last checkup, the doctor discovered she had high blood pressure. She's been on medication to control it for several months now," Whit explained.

"Why wasn't I told? I didn't know." The words came out in a sob.

"She probably didn't want to worry you. It's immaterial now," he stated logically.

"It's my fault." She leaned against him, guilt pressing at her. "I should have gone home on my vacation instead of coming here. When I talked to her tonight, I should have told her I was coming instead of stalling and making her wonder why I wasn't." She blamed herself for being thoughtless.

"Elizabeth was worried about Rory, too," Whit reminded her.

At the moment, she was only concerned about her own guilt. "I'll never forgive myself if anything happens to her." Her face was hidden in the curve of his neck.

His arms tightened around her in silent comfort while his hand stroked the back of her hair. "She'll be all right, Shari." His mouth formed the words against her temple. "You'll see."

Despite his assurance, she shuddered against him. "I'm so scared," Shari whispered and her lips brushed against the warm feel of his skin.

He seemed to withdraw his comfort, first mentally, then physically as he took hold of her shoulders and forced her to stand away from him. That wasn't what she wanted, but in her weakened state, she couldn't resist him.

"There isn't time for that, Shari." His voice was hard and inflexible. Its lack of sympathy hurt her.

The sound of heavy footsteps briefly distracted her and she turned her head in their direction. Rory was coming down the steps, yawning widely, his black hair all tousled from sleep.

"What's going on?" he asked sleepily. "Who was at the door?"

"It's Mother," Shari answered him without thinking about the shock the news would be to him.

Whit stepped in before she cruelly blurted out the words. "There's some bad news from home, Rory." He gave Rory a minute to brace himself. "Two State Patrol officers came to inform us that your mother has had a stroke and we're wanted at home immediately."

"Oh, no." He leaned against the stair railing, choking up. "How bad . . . is she?"

"We don't know," Whit admitted. "I suggest we don't waste any more time talking about it. You two need to get your things packed so we can leave as soon as you're ready."

"Yes." Rory was already turning to climb the stairs, his head downcast under his own weight of guilt.

"You, too, Shari." Whit pointed her in the direction of the stairs, prodding her along. "I'll let your friends know about the situation and give them a key so they can stay here as long as they like."

"Yes," she murmured because she had forgotten all about Beth and Doré. With the news about her mother, their vacation plans were thrown to the winds.

Once Shari was alone in her room, shock seemed to take over. She stood in its center, looking at nothing, forgetting even why she was there. A few minutes later, Beth came in to help her pack and laid out a set of clothes for Shari to wear. With the help of her friend, Shari managed to be dressed and packed by the time Whit came to her room.

"Are you positive you're going to be all right, Shari?" Beth asked anxiously as Whit picked up the suitcase to carry it downstairs. "I'll come with you."

"No." Shari smiled wanly at the generous offer. "You and Doré stay here and enjoy your vacation. I'll be okay."

"I'll look after her," Whit promised, tucking a hand under her arm to usher Shari out of the door.

Doré was waiting at the head of the stairs. Their earlier disagreement was forgotten as she hugged Shari and tried to offer words of encouragement and hope. But it was the expression of friendship more than what she said that Shari remembered.

It was a silent trio that climbed into Whit's car parked outside the condominium. Earlier that day, Shari had dreaded the thought of returning to Gold Leaf, but she couldn't get there fast enough now.

She sat in the passenger seat in front with Whit, and Rory hid in the shadowed darkness of the back. Her younger brother hadn't said a word since he'd asked the one question about their mother's condition. It seemed to take forever on the winding roads before they left the mountains behind and began driving on the high plateau of the piedmont region.

"How much longer?" Shari finally put the question to Whit, unable to contain the impatience born of anxiety any longer.

"Another hour—hopefully less if the traffic stays light," he answered shortly.

A moan came from the backseat, a kind of protest to the time still ahead of them without any news.

"None of this would have happened if I'd left Mom a note," Rory declared in a voice heavy with self-recrimination. "I was so busy thinking about myself, I didn't give a thought about what this would do to her."

"I'm guilty, too." Shari wouldn't let him take the full blame.

"It's spilt milk now," Whit inserted curtly. "It isn't going to help Elizabeth to have you two wallowing in guilt when she sees you."

No matter how wise it was, it was difficult advice to accept. "She's too young to have something like this happen to her," Shari protested.

"It's happened," Whit stated as proof she wasn't too young.

His lack of sympathy with their guilt ended any further conversation before it began. If Whit hadn't been there, Shari was certain she and Rory would have talked themselves into a state of abject misery.

The golden glow of daybreak was on the eastern horizon when they neared their destination. Shari expected Whit to drive directly to the hospital. She was confused when he took the turnoff to the family home.

"Aren't you taking us to the hospital?" she frowned.

"No. We're going home first and find out what the situation is," he stated in that tone of authority that didn't listen to arguments contrary to his decision.

"But we can find out there," Rory leaned forward to protest.

"Before either of you see your mother, you're going to shower and clean up." His gaze skimmed Shari's pale and drawn features with a critical eye. "There's no need for her to be worrying about your health."

Neither of them argued with that. They were already weighed down with enough guilt not to want more. Besides, Gold Leaf wasn't far away now, so they'd be finding out how she was soon.

A little ache welled in Shari's throat at the sight of the familiar green tobacco fields and the drying sheds. When she caught the first glimpse of the old pillared mansion standing so proudly in the morning light, a tear slipped from her lashes. She wasn't a Lancaster so it didn't belong to her, but it was where she had lived as a child.

All her memories were wrapped around that house and this land. It affected her this way every time she came back, but the homecoming never lasted longer than her first meeting with Granddad Lancaster, Shari hoped he was at the hospital, and this one time, her homecoming wouldn't be spoiled by angry words.

Whit parked the car at the head of the circular drive near the porticoed front entrance. A carriage house in the rear of the old mansion had long ago been converted into a garage, but there was no point in driving the car back there when they'd be leaving soon.

There wasn't any standing on ceremony as all three climbed out as soon as the motor was switched off. Shari waited by the steps while Rory and Whit took the suitcases out of the trunk of the car. She turned loving eyes on the massive structure, its white walls rising two and a half stories into the air. It was built to withstand time and the elements, a fitting home for the Lancaster dynasty.

At the approach of her half brother and stepbrother, Shari climbed the steps to the front door. The knob yielded to the touch of her hand and she pushed it open to walk inside. It had always seemed that nothing could happen within these thick walls without the direct permission of a Lancaster, which made it all the more difficult to accept that her mother had been stricken and was lying in a hospital bed. Perhaps the Lancasters weren't so omnipotent after all.

The wide hallway echoed their footsteps on the oak floors, an intrusion in the silence. Soon it was answered by another set of footsteps hurrying toward the front hallway. The housekeeper, Mrs. Youngblood, appeared, relief breaking through her strained expression when she saw them.

"Thank God you've arrived." It was truly a prayer of thanks by the religious woman as she sent a glance heavenward.

"How's Mother?" Shari asked the question uppermost in her mind as a door to her left was opened.

It led to the library, the private sanctuary of Lancaster males. Shari stiffened and half-turned to look at the aged man she knew would be standing in the opening. Frederick Lancaster leaned heavily on his cane, an indication that his health wasn't as robust as his body appeared.

His height was equal to Whit's, but advanced years had stooped him. His dark hair had turned to an iron shade of gray and a multitude of lines had weathered his face. However, his eyes burned brightly with the topaz color she often saw reflected in Whit's.

Mrs. Youngblood didn't offer any information now that the head of the family was on the scene. She left it to Frederick Lancaster to inform them of Elizabeth Sutherland Lancaster's present condition.

"So, Whit has brought the runaway children home," he commented with an edge of reproval.

"He didn't bring us home. We came," Shari corrected, bristling as she always did when she confronted him. "How is Mother?"

"You've never been concerned about her before this," he pointed out. "Isn't it a bit hypocritical to come rushing back when she's in the hospital?"

"They're here now, Granddad," Whit inserted firmly. "That's all that's necessary for the present. What is Elizabeth's condition?"

"She has had a bad stroke, but the doctors are confident that she will recover." His cane thumped the hardwood floor as he hobbled into the entrance hall.

The first tingle of relief went through Shari and her glance ran to Rory to share the moment. He blinked at the tears in his eyes, trying not to let them be seen lest his grandfather think he was weak.

"I'm taking Shari and Rory to the hospital to see her as soon as they've freshened up and changed," Whit stated.

"I'll never understand how a woman as selfless as Elizabeth could have two such thoughtless children," their grandfather declared in open disgust. "All you care about is yourselves."

"That isn't true," Shari angrily denied the charge.

"What do you think started this all off?" he challenged. "Rory goes tearing off to join the circus. He didn't even have the courtesy to leave a note to explain why he was leaving—or the guts to tell us he was going."

"This wasn't Rory's fault," Shari insisted as her younger brother paled under the accusation of blame.

"You're damn right it wasn't!" the patriarch of the Lancaster family agreed with an emphatic nod, and pointed an arthritically crooked finger at Shari. "It was yours! He was only doing what he knew you did at his age! I should never have listened to Whit. I should have hauled you back here and locked you in your room."

"You couldn't have kept me here! Not you! Not anybody!" She was shouting. She hadn't been inside the house a minute before she was locked in another one of their duels of will.

"After all your mother did for you, I'll never understand how you could treat her the way you have," he said coldly. "You don't even come to see her during the college breaks unless you have nothing better to do."

"And just why do you think I stay away from Gold Leaf?" Shari stormed. "It's because of you! You think you can control everybody's life. You want everybody to do what you want! That's why I left—and that's why Rory left! We just couldn't stand it any more! If anyone's to blame for what happened to Mother, it's you!"

"Shari, that's enough!" Whit ordered.

There were hot tears in her green eyes when she looked at him. "I don't know why I let you bring me here! I knew this would happen!"

"I brought you here because this is your home," he stated.

"No, it isn't! It's never been my home. I only lived here," she retorted, speaking the truth she had always felt. "It belongs to Lancasters and I'm a Sutherland. I used to cry myself to sleep at night because I wasn't a Lancaster. But when I look at you—" She turned to her step-grandfather, "—I'm glad I'm not! I'm glad!"

Before she disgraced herself by breaking into tears, Shari bolted for the stairs, brushing past the embarrassed housekeeper who had been an unwilling witness to the bitter exchange. She ran directly to the room that had always been hers and threw herself onto the bed, sobbing openly.

Someone touched her shoulder. She stirred, peering tearily through her lashes to see Whit standing by her bed.

"Go away," she complained.

"Take a shower and run some cold water over your face," he instructed. "You don't want your mother to see that you've been crying when we go to the hospital.''

It was true. She didn't. She managed to restrain her sobs to hiccoughing sounds. ''Why does he always have to do this to me?''

''Believe it or not, he loves you, Shari,'' Whit answered. ''Now get a move on. We're leaving for the hospital in twenty minutes. You don't have much time to get ready.''

CHAPTER FIVE

COLD WATER took a lot of the puffiness out of her face, but not all of it. Exactly twenty minutes from the time Whit had given her, Shari was descending the steps. She paused at the landing, rawly stiffening when she saw her grandfather waiting at the bottom, using the banister for support instead of his cane.

Determined not to let him incite her to anger again, Shari started down the steps. Her emotions were too torn apart from the sequence of recent events to endure another battle royal with him.

"Shari," he called her name when she would have walked right past him. She would have done so anyway if she hadn't heard a placating quality in his voice. So she stopped and turned to look at him, a vaguely defiant tilt to her chin.

"Yes."

"I was upset and probably said some things I shouldn't have." His reply came close to a grudging apology, but he was too proud to come right out and say he had been wrong. "Your mother's illness has been a strain on all of us, I guess."

"Yes," she admitted that her nerves had been worn thin by it.

"You've been like my own granddaughter. I've always wanted you to regard Gold Leaf as your home," he insisted.

"I've explained how I feel about that." Shari avoided his gaze.

"Yes," he sighed heavily and paused. "We both have a bit of a hot temper. Do you think we could manage to observe a truce—for your mother's sake?"

Coming from him, it was quite a gesture. "I think we could try." Shari was moved to agree.

He offered to shake hands on the bargain and Shari accepted. He held her hand an instant longer. "If I interfere too much—" he said without admitting that he did. "—it's only because I want you to do what is best."

"Best, according to your standards," she reminded him.

"Yes...well...." He released her hand, unwilling to go so far as to admit that there were standards other than his own. "Whit is waiting outside for you. You'd better go. Give Elizabeth my love."

"I will," Shari promised and hurried down the hallway to the front door.

Whit had the engine running when she climbed into the empty passenger seat of the car. He ran a glance over her before shifting gears to start down the drive. Rory was in the backseat.

"Did you talk to Granddad?" Whit inquired with apparent foreknowledge that she had.

"Yes." She suspected he had had something to do with it. "We agreed to a truce of sorts."

"He could use some compassion from you," Whit stated.

"Why?" She asked the question to discover Whit's reason for saying that, not to argue whether or not it was true.

"Granddad has buried his parents, his brothers, his wife, and his son. Your mother may be his daughter-in-law, but he has developed a deep affection for her over the years.

He had to have been very worried and frightened when she had the stroke. Try to imagine how helpless he felt at the time," Whit suggested with a side glance at her. "And the three of us weren't there. He needed us as much as your mother did—perhaps more."

Helpless, frightened—those weren't words Shari would have associated with Frederick Lancaster. He was the strong, stern head of the family. In the space of twenty-four hours, her entire outlook on things seemed to have turned topsy-turvy.

"I suppose he did," Shari conceded the possibility.

"Whit talked to Annie," Rory spoke up from the backseat, referring to the housekeeper by her given name. "Mom is partially paralyzed from the stroke."

Her widened gaze flew to Whit in alarm. "Is that true?" she asked in a small voice.

"Yes," he admitted without taking his attention from the road, and speaking very matter-of-factly. "Her left side has been affected. Her speech has been impaired."

"Not permanently?" Shari hoped fervently.

"No," Whit confirmed. "At this point, the doctors can't say how much use she'll recover or how soon. It's going to be a long, slow process."

Shari sank back in her seat. "I hadn't thought...I hadn't realized..." she murmured.

"It's better if you know all this before you see her," Whit stated. "Both of you need to be prepared for the way she's going to look and act."

"Yes," she agreed numbly.

His advice proved to be invaluable. Without it, Shari was certain she would have broken down and cried when she saw her mother lying in the hospital bed, so incapacitated and unable to communicate. The smile Shari plastered on her face never cracked under the strain of maintaining a cheerful front. It remained in place until she stepped out of the room, and a raw shudder shook it away.

"Are you okay?" Whit was beside her, a hand on her waist in a silent offer of support if she needed it.

"Yes," she nodded affirmatively and breathed in deeply. Lifting her head, Shari studied his handsomely carved features and the compassion written in his amber-brown eyes. "I want to stay with her." She expected him to argue, so she rushed to justify her request. "I know she's receiving excellent care from the hospital staff, but they're all strangers to her. It would be less of an ordeal if she could see a familiar face."

"You don't need to convince me, Shari," Whit smiled faintly, the sun-creased lines deepening around his eyes. "I agree."

"You do?" She was vaguely surprised, although she wasn't sure why.

"A member of the family should sit with her. I know she'll be very pleased if that person is you. She's missed you a great deal since you've been away at college. We all have," he added with an intently probing look.

There was a tightness in her throat. She made a little move toward him. A second later, he was taking her into his arms to hold her close and rest a hard cheek against her hair. Shari reveled in the strength and comfort she found in his undemanding embrace. His hand gently rubbed her shoulder blade, his touch familiar yet with a trace of intimacy.

"You belong at Gold Leaf," Whit muttered near her ear, his warm breath stirring her hair. "It is your home, Shari. Someday I'll prove it to you."

Something unsettled her. She was too confused to decipher whether it was his subject matter or the hard flesh and bone of his male body pressed to her length. Whit seemed to sense the beginnings of resistance in her and loosened the circle of his arms to let her stand alone. There seemed to be a veil over his expression, yet there wasn't anything different in the way he looked at her.

A nurse walked by them in the corridor, her white uniform rustling softly. Shari was reminded of where they were and why. Concern for her mother overrode the vague confusion of the moment.

"I'll let Mother know I'll be staying with her," she said.

"Just during the day," Whit qualified. "After visiting hours are over at night, you'll be coming home to Gold Leaf."

That day started a routine that was followed for an entire week. Shari spent the daylight hours at her mother's side and drove back to Gold Leaf late in the evenings to sleep. In one short week, her mother had made a lot of progress.

From not being able to make any intelligible sound at all that first day, she could make understandable words. It was still difficult for her to speak in complete sentences, so their conversation usually included a sign language they had developed. She had recovered some use of her left side, and the doctors hoped she would regain more of it with physical therapy.

After witnessing some of the minor triumphs her mother had achieved, Shari was encouraged by her progress. Her mother would definitely get better.

She told Beth that when her friend phoned on a Friday morning before Shari had left for the hospital. "The doctors are talking about releasing her next week," she added.

"Shari, I'm so glad to hear it," her friend declared.

"We all are." It was a tremendous relief.

"Doré and I are back at the sorority house. Will you be arriving Sunday?" Beth asked. "Don't forget classes start again on Monday morning."

"I wish I could," Shari smiled ruefully. "I suppose I'll come sometime late Sunday night."

"We'll be watching for you," she promised. Let us know if there is any change in your plans—and drive carefully."

"I will."

There was an exchange of good-byes before Shari hung up the telephone receiver. She glanced at her watch and saw she was running late. A cup of coffee and some toast were all she'd have time to have for breakfast this morning. She wasn't worried about being hungry before lunch because she could always get some scrambled eggs and sausage at the hospital cafeteria.

When she entered the dining room, Rory and her grandfather were seated at the mahogany table. Whit had eaten breakfast hours ago and was already gone. She hadn't seen much of her stepbrother this past week, except for a short time in the evenings or when he visited her mother at the hospital.

"Who were you talking to on the phone?" Frederick Lancaster questioned as he dabbed a spoonful of marmalade on his toast.

"Beth Daniels, one of my friends from Duke," Shari answered and smothered the rise of irritation. Her step-grandfather considered anything that went on in this house his business. He didn't regard such inquiries as an invasion of privacy.

Their truce was still in effect. That it had lasted so long was due to the prolonged time Shari spent at the hospital. She was certain of that.

"What did she want?" he demanded as Shari poured a cup of coffee from the silver pot on the table.

"To see how Mom was getting along," she replied. "And to find out when I would be coming back. Classes start on Monday."

"You aren't going."

The piece of toast in her hand was halted midway to her mouth as her startled gaze swung to the elderly man seated at the head of the table. She played the words back in her mind to see if there had been any element of a question in the way he said them. There wasn't. And there was nothing in his expression to indicate he expected a reply from her. Frederick Lancaster had handed down another one of his edicts and expected her to accept it.

"I'm not going where?" Shari set the toast on her plate and stubbornly dug in her heels, too independent to be dictated to by him.

"You're not going back to college." He repeated his statement with determination. "You're here and you are staying here until your mother has fully recovered."

"I am leaving Sunday for college," she stated firmly. "There is absolutely no reason to stay longer. Mom isn't in any danger. She'll be released from the hospital next week. With you, Whit, Rory and Mrs. Youngblood all here, she'll have plenty of company. I don't have to be here, too."

"You are actually considering going back," her step-grandfather challenged as if she had taken leave of her senses. "Have you any idea how much your mother worries about you? She's doing fine now, but what if she has a relapse because of you? Do you want that on your conscience?"

"That's blackmail," Shari accused.

"Call it what you like," Frederick Lancaster declared. "After all your mother has done for you, this is one thing you can do for her. You can be here when she needs you."

"I have been here when she needed me," Shari insisted.

"One week out of how many?" he taunted. "Is that an even trade? If your education means so much to you—more than your mother—then transfer to a college closer where you can commute daily from Gold Leaf."

"That's what you really want, isn't it?" she challenged bitterly. "You want me back under your thumb."

"I want you here with your mother where you belong!" he retorted. "Postpone returning to the university until the fall semester. Or is that too much to ask, too?"

"You don't *ask!*" Shari stormed, rising from the table without touching her toast or coffee. "You *order!* But you aren't ordering me."

Her long-legged strides carried her out of the room in high temper. "Come back here!" Frederick Lancaster ordered. But Shari ignored the command.

She didn't stop until she was outside and behind the wheel of her small sports car.

Leaning one arm on the steering wheel, she raked a hand through the thick mass of her raven hair in frustration. She should have known the truce wouldn't last, but she had wanted it to so badly.

The front door opened and Shari immediately started the car's engine, thinking it was Granddad Lancaster. But it was Rory who ran down the steps to the car.

"Sis, where are you going?" Anxiety was written in his young face as he bent down to look in the car window.

"To the hospital." Furrows of inner impatience and anger continued to crease her forehead.

"Don't go back to college," he pleaded.

She stared at him in silent shock. "You surely don't expect me to give in to his blackmail!"

"I don't know." There was a quiet desperation in the way he moved his head to the side, a helpless gesture of someone at his wit's end. "If you aren't here, I don't know whether I can take it. How can I stay if you go?"

"Don't put all this on me," Shari protested. It wasn't fair to make her responsible for his actions but that was precisely what

Rory was doing. The emotional blackmail was coming at her from another member of the family.

"You're the only one who understands," Rory persisted. "Please, don't go back."

There was too much pressure. She lowered her head for an instant. "I don't know what I'm going to do." Shari sighed heavily and looked out the car's windshield with troubled green eyes. "I've got to go, or Mom will be wondering where I am." She shifted the car out of neutral gear into drive, and Rory stepped back.

Shari had a lot of time to think during the drive to the hospital, but her thoughts were no clearer when she arrived. Her mother seemed to be in exceptionally good spirits, which gave Shari a little boost.

A couple of her mother's friends stopped by to visit her. Shari waited until they had left before attempting to bring the conversation around to her imminent departure for college. If her mother took the news well, then the pressure from her grandfather would be negated. At least, that's what Shari hoped.

"Did I tell you Beth Daniels called this morning to see how you were?" she asked brightly and saw the vagueness in her mother's eyes that indicated the name wasn't familiar to her. "You've heard me talk about Beth," Shari reminded her mother. "She and I are in the same sorority at college. Beth, myself, and Doré Evans were spending our vacation together when you had your stroke."

There was a movement of the woman's head on the pillow as she recalled the name. Shari reached out to link her fingers with her mother's right hand in a kind of reassurance.

"Anyway, I told Beth how much better you are, improving by leaps and bounds every day," Shari smiled in silent encouragement.

"I'm ... try ... ing." Her mother had to speak slowly, and carefully form the words to make them come out right.

"You are succeeding," Shari insisted and paused before breaking the news to her mother. "Beth was concerned that I wouldn't be able to make it back for the start of classes Monday morning, but I explained you would be released next week so there wasn't any reason for me to delay coming back."

"N...no." Her mother frantically tried to get her message across, tightening her hold on Shari's hand as if to keep Shari at her side.

Shari felt the wrenching of her heartstrings and tried to conceal how her mother's distress was affecting her. "You'll be all right," she assured her, more confidently than she felt. "You'll be home soon with Granddad, Whit, and Rory. Mrs. Youngblood will spoil you terribly."

Her mother became very agitated which only hampered her ability to talk. "M... m...miss...you."

"I'll miss you, too," Shari insisted. "But I'm only a phone call away. I can come home on the weekends to see you. That really isn't so bad, is it?" she reasoned, but her mother wasn't convinced.

Granddad Lancaster's warning kept ringing in her ears—what if she has a relapse? Shari tried desperately to calm her mother down and make sense of the mumbled words she was saying without much success. There were tears in her mother's eyes and a mist was forming in Shari's emerald pair.

She was about to ring for a nurse when she heard a set of footsteps approach the private room. She recognized that easy striding walk immediately. Relief trembled through her when Whit appeared in the doorway. His sweeping glance quickly assessed the situation.

"What's going on here?" Although his voice was light, his gaze was sharp as he walked to the hospital bed. There was a gentleness about his expression that enhanced his innate strength.

"Mom became upset when I mentioned I was due back at college Monday for classes," Shari explained, because her mother was too agitated to make herself understood. "I've told her she'll be all right."

Whit rested a hand on Shari's shoulder, but kept his attention centered on her mother. A smile of understanding curved his mouth.

"You don't want Shari to go back, is that it?" he asked. Her mother relaxed a little and nodded with slight relief. "I'll have a talk with her," he promised and her mother cast an anxious glance at Shari. "Will you trust me to handle this, Elizabeth?" Whit asked.

There was a hesitation before her mother agreed with a small nod of her head. "Yes," she said clearly and appeared considerably reassured.

Shari marveled at how quickly Whit had brought the situation under control. He had only promised to talk to her, not guaranteeing the results, yet her mother was satisfied. Shari conceded that he definitely had a way about him that inspired confidence.

His hand tightened on her shoulder, but when he spoke, it was addressed to her mother. "I'm going to buy Shari a cup of coffee. I'll be back later to see you."

The pressure of his hand prompted Shari to stand. "We won't be gone long," she promised her mother and allowed Whit to escort her from the room.

As they walked down the corridor, Shari slanted a look at his chiseled profile. She liked its strength and the straight bridge of his nose, the intelligent slant of his forehead and the slight thrust of his chin. His hair was the color of burley tobacco, vitally thick and styled with masculine carelessness.

When his downward glance intercepted her study of him, Shari tried to hide the interest that had been strictly feminine. "I don't know how you did it," she declared with a disbelieving shake of her head.

"Did what?" Whit asked.

"Pacified Mother," she replied. "You are more effective than a sedative."

A throaty chuckle came from him, its rich, deep sound warm with humor. "I don't know if I like being told I put people to sleep."

"Ah, but only if that's what you want them to do," Shari qualified the statement, a dark brow arching with amusement.

"Do you have any suggestions how I might go about persuading you to wait until the fall term to go back to college?" Whit inquired with seeming humor, but underneath, he was quite serious.

Shari lowered her gaze to the tiled floor of the hospital corridor, all her defenses leaping into place. "Don't you start in on me, too, Whit," she asked grimly. "I'm not sure I can take it. First, it was Granddad, then Rory, then Mom, and now you. Why do you have to gang up on me like this?"

"Haven't you got the message yet?" he asked quietly. "We are all lost without you, Shari. Gold Leaf doesn't seem alive if you aren't there."

Whit sounded so serious, as if he truly meant every word he was saying. Shari was forced to meet the dark intensity of his gaze. She couldn't believe she was that important to all of them, yet the insistence was there in his eyes.

Stopping, Whit drew her to the side of the corridor out of the traffic area. She faced him, uncertain about his reason for halting. One had continued to rest on the curve of her waist while his other hand smoothed the hair away from her cheek and stayed to hold her face.

The action was so close to a caress there was a little race of her pulse. If any other man than Whit had done it, Shari would have regarded it as such.

"Have I ever asked you to do anything for me?" Whit murmured the husky challenge.

The way he was looking at her made everything else seem unimportant. "No," she admitted, disturbed by the softness of her answer.

"Then, I'm asking you now—for me. Stay with us at Gold Leaf until the fall term begins?" His steady gaze continued to weave its spell over her.

She breathed in, trying to find the willful stubbornness that had seen her through the confrontations with the other members of her family but it wasn't there. She was powerless to refuse him.

"I'll stay." Shari released the indrawn breath in a sigh of surrender to a force she couldn't identify or combat. Her troubled green eyes searched the rugged, male contours of Whit's face, trying to discover why he had succeeded when the others had failed.

"Thank you." He bent his head toward her.

For a split second, Shari was startled by the warmth of his male lips against hers. Something was wrong with her reaction to the innocent kiss. Little quivers of delight were running through her.

In a completely involuntary action, her lips softened and moved against his to invite a more complete demonstration of his affection. Just for an instant, Shari felt his mouth harden in response, then Whit was pulling away.

"I promised you a cup of coffee, didn't I?" There was a certain briskness in his reminder while a degree of aloofness had entered his expression.

Shari desperately tried to match it. "Yes, you did." She didn't want him to guess that

his brotherly kiss of gratitude had been misinterpreted.

They resumed their course to the cafeteria.
Over a cup of coffee, they discussed only
general topics. No reference was made to her
decision to stay at Gold Leaf for the rest of
the summer—or to the brief kiss that she had
nearly made into something more.

When they returned to her mother's room,
Whit informed Elizabeth that Shari had
agreed to stay at Gold Leaf and return to college for the fall semester, but he didn't make
a momentous occasion out of it. He treated it
as a simple thing and, thus, prevented her
mother from making a big fuss over it. After
chatting with her for twenty minutes, Whit
excused himself, explaining he was needed at
Gold Leaf.

After he'd gone, Shari read to her mother
for a while. Nothing was said about her decision to stay. It was as if she had never mentioned leaving. Shari let the pretense stand.
She didn't want to think about how easily she
had given in to Whit's subtle persuasion.

That evening, she arrived at Gold Leaf just
as the family was sitting down to dinner. Whit
stood to pull out the chair next to his, invit-

ing her to join them. Shari hesitated, then sat down. When she caught the relieved look in Rory's eyes, she knew Whit had informed them that she was staying for the summer.

"I had a sandwich at the hospital so I'm not very hungry," she warned the elderly man at the head of the table.

Lancaster tradition dictated that the head of the table dish out the portions. He nodded a silent acknowledgement and continued ladling the peanut soup from its tureen into individual cups.

"How was Mom today?" Rory asked.

"Very good." Shari took the cup of soup Whit passed to her and noticed it was only half-full. "Doctor Ellis was in this afternoon and said if she kept it up, she could come home on Monday."

Throughout the meal, it seemed to Shari that everyone was determined to avoid any subject that might be controversial. Even Rory managed to revert to his old teasing ways. It was the most pleasant dinner she had enjoyed at Gold Leaf in a long time.

When Mrs. Youngblood carried in a tray with individual servings of peach cobbler, Shari folded her napkin and laid it beside her place setting. "None for me, thank you," she refused and glanced at her watch. "I need to call Beth and let her know not to expect me on Sunday."

"That isn't necessary," Granddad Lancaster spoke up. "I have already contacted the college and your sorority to inform them that you wouldn't be returning until the fall."

Shari was stunned, an anger building. "And who gave you the right to do that?" she demanded.

"It's done, Shari." Whit attempted to calm her down with a quiet word and a silencing look.

"It's done." She angrily taunted him with his own phrase. "And I'm supposed to accept it."

"There's very little you can do about it now," he pointed out.

"That's what Granddad counted on," she retorted and flashed a rebellious look at the instigator of the scene. "You think you can run everybody's life, don't you?" Shari challenged. "Well, you're not running mine!"

"I was merely saving you the trouble—" Frederick Lancaster began.

"No you weren't! You were making trouble! You always make trouble!" she raged and abruptly stood up, nearly knocking her chair over.

She wanted to throw something at him but she knew that was wrong. Pivoting away from the table, Shari walked quickly from the room and headed directly for the staircase. She seethed in a low fury as she climbed the stairs to seek the privacy of her room.

Angered that she had ever agreed to stay, Shari swept into her room and obeyed the impulse to lock her door. With her hands clenched into fists, she walked to the second-story window and stared through the glass panes at the sheds and bulk barns for storing Gold Leaf tobacco. Beyond the plantation buildings were the rolling fields of leggy tobacco plants, coloring the ground with a deep shade of green.

In the outer hallway, footsteps approached her door. Shari stiffened and glanced warily over her shoulder, fires of resentment still burning green in her eyes. The doorknob was tried but its locked bolt resisted the attempt. A trio of summoning knocks followed each other in rapid succession.

"Shari, open the door." Whit's firm voice was slightly muffled by the separating panel of the heavy door.

"Leave me alone," she replied. "I don't want to talk to you."

She didn't want him to reason away her anger. She had a right to feel outraged at the way the patriarch of the Lancaster family had taken it upon himself to handle her affairs.

"You're acting like a child." His voice was curt with impatience. "Unlock this door."

His accusation that her behavior was childish prompted Shari to take a step toward the door. She stopped the instant she realized that had been his intention.

"I will not," Shari stated to let him know she wouldn't be coerced.

"All right. Just stay in there and pout," Whit replied grimly.

He didn't give her a chance to change her mind. Shari heard his footsteps carry him away from her door the minute he had finished speaking. She was left with the uncomfortable sensation that she hadn't handled the scene very well. There was a vague irritation with herself that she couldn't quite shake.

It became a silly matter of pride that kept her in the room the rest of the evening. To pass the time, Shari made a project out of bathing and washing her hair. Finally she was left with nothing else to do but get ready for bed.

Lying beneath the covers, she listened to the male members of the Lancaster family turning in for the night. Whit's room was next to hers. The dividing walls partially muffled the sounds of him moving about. Finally the house was silent. She closed her eyes but she wasn't even close to being sleepy.

CHAPTER SIX

ALONE IN her bedroom, Shari felt isolated and adrift. Memories of long-ago nights crowded into her mind—the innocent, midnight chats in Whit's room. She longed for that comfortable relationship when she had been able to talk over her problems, big or small, with Whit.

Those had been special times, precious moments to look back on with fondness. There was a desire to reach back into the past and make it part of the present.

Throwing aside her covers, she climbed out of bed and pulled on a robe over her shortie pajamas. There wasn't any need for a light as Shari made her way to the door and unlocked it. She knew her way around the house blindfolded.

Her bare feet made hardly any sound in the carpeted hallway. Not wanting to waken the other members of the household, Shari went directly to Whit's door. A sliver of light shone beneath it, letting her know he wasn't yet asleep. She knocked softly. Obeying old habits, she opened the door a crack without waiting for permission to enter.

"It's me," Shari whispered when she saw him sitting up in bed, smoking a cigarette. "Can I come in?"

"It's late," he reminded her without actually telling her she couldn't.

"I know." She slipped inside his room and quietly closed the door.

The only light in his room came from the lamp on his bedside table. Its pool of light illuminated the man in bed, propped into a sitting position by a pair of pillows. A blanket and sheet covered the lower half of his body, but his naked chest was exposed to her view, a dark circling of hairs in its center. It wasn't an uncommon sight. Shari remembered from past occasions that Whit had a habit of sleeping in his undershorts.

It had never bothered her before to see the sinewed expanse of his naked shoulders and the muscled flatness of his stomach. She tried to ignore the vague disturbance that wandered through her system this time.

"Maybe I should follow your lead and start locking my door," Whit suggested when she approached his bed.

"I wasn't in the mood to talk," she offered in the way of an indirect apology for locking him out of her room earlier that night. "You shouldn't smoke in bed," Shari criticized to change the subject.

"I believe you've warned me about that before." He crushed the cigarette butt in the glass ashtray on the nightstand. Several others already occupied the ashtray along with a collection of ashes.

"Obviously you don't pay attention," she observed. "I guess you take after your grandfather. He does what he wants regardless of what other people say."

"When are you going to grow up and realize he's an old man." Whit didn't show any sympathy for her position. "Do you have any idea what it cost him to turn over the management of Gold Leaf to me because he wasn't capable of running it anymore?"

"I'm sure it was difficult for him," Shari conceded grudgingly.

"Difficult? It nearly killed him." His reply was flat. "He has tried to compensate for that loss by asserting authority over you and Rory. He wants to be important so he takes things upon himself to fill that need.''

Shari knew she had never considered the situation in that light, but it was hard for her to admit it. She had a stubborn streak that ran a mile wide.

''That's easy for you to say. It isn't your life he's trying to run,'' she retorted, then sighed. ''I try not to lose my temper with him but I always do.''

''Have you ever tried counting to ten?'' Whit suggested dryly, evoking a smile from her.

''No, Granddad would suspect that I can't count that high.'' Shari grinned and pushed at long, blanket-covered mounds where his legs were. ''Move over so I can sit down.''

Something hard flashed in his eyes as he shifted his position to make room for her. ''Don't you think you're too old to be climbing into my bed in the middle of the night?'' Whit challenged.

Shari didn't take his question seriously and climbed onto his bed to sit cross-legged facing him. ''I've missed those long talks we used to have on this bed.''

Her glance wandered around the room, touching on familiar objects like the photograph of his parents on the dresser and a later, family portrait that included her mother, Rory, and herself. A hooked rug continued to occupy the center of the room, protecting the hardwood floor. Time had changed little about the room, outside of a few new books on the shelf above the desk.

"One of the best things that ever happened to me was when my mother married John Lancaster and you became my brother, Whit," she declared, bringing her gaze back to him.

But his attention was focused on the ruffled neckline of her pajama top where it dipped low to reveal the swell of her breasts. There was sharp, almost angry, reproval in his glance when it lifted to her face.

"Why did you bother to wear a robe?" he challenged.

A little embarrassed by her inadvertent lack of modesty, Shari fumbled for the loose ends of the robe's sash. "I guess I just forgot to tie it." She quickly corrected that omission, crossing the front folds of the robe over each other and securing them with a knot in the cloth belt.

"I think it's time you were going back to your own room," Whit stated with a thin-lipped expression.

"Not yet," Shari protested. "We've hardly had a chance to talk."

"Then get up," he ordered. "If we're going to talk, it's going to be somewhere other than this bed."

Although puzzled by his behavior, she uncurled her legs and slid off the bed to the floor. The bed had always been the location for their talks. She didn't understand why he was suddenly changing the routine.

"Hand me my pants," Whit ordered. "They're lying on that chair over there." Shari walked to the straight-backed chair he had indicated and started to pick up the pair of tan denims draped across the seat. "I've got stuff in the pockets," he warned her not to let it fall out.

She picked them up by the waistband and carried them to the bed. "Here you are." She handed them over to him.

Whit remained under the covers, holding the pants in his hand and looking at her expectantly. But Shari didn't know what he expected from her. The corners of his mouth were pulled inward in an expression of exhausted patience.

"Will you please turn around?" he requested with a circling gesture of his hand, a trace of harshness in his tone.

She released a short laugh of surprise. "Are you serious?" she asked, unable to keep the laughter out of her voice. "Whit, I've seen you in your undershorts before."

But he didn't find anything funny about the situation. If anything, his expression became harder and more forbidding.

"Dammit, I said turn around," he snapped.

Bewildered over the reason for his anger, Shari did as she was told and faced away from the bed. His attitude seemed to change the entire atmosphere in the room. She was much more conscious of the sounds he was making behind her—the muted clink of the coins in his pockets as he pulled on his pants and the zip of the fly closing. It started a lot of disturbing thoughts.

She tried to eliminate them by making light of the situation. "When did you become so shy, Whit?'' she asked, very careful not to turn her head. ''I don't remember modesty being one of your virtues.''

There was an impatient click of a cigarette lighter. Out of the corner of her eye, Shari caught the swirl of tobacco smoke. Then Whit was briskly walking by her toward the chairs on the other side of the room. He stopped when he realized she wasn't following him and looked back at her.

''You said you wanted to talk,'' he reminded her curtly. ''Let's talk.''

''What is the matter with you, Whit?'' She was drawn slowly in his direction, her gaze searching the taut features for an explanation for his strange behavior. ''You aren't acting like yourself at all.''

''Oh?'' The simple sound bordered on a taunting challenge. ''Perhaps you should enlighten me on the proper way I should behave.'' He had just lit the cigarette and already he was turning to put it out, using an ashtray on the desk. ''Just exactly what is it that you expect from me?''

''I guess I expect you to act more like the Whit I remember.'' Shari wasn't certain herself.

"Times change—and people with them,"
he answered curtly.

"Maybe so," she shrugged. "But you're
still my brother."

Something seemed to snap in him. The anger that had been held in check suddenly
erupted. Shari blinked in shock when he
roughly grabbed her arms and gave her a hard
shake. A dark fury raged in his hard eyes.

"Dammit, I am not your brother!" His
voice was husky with his effort to keep its
volume down. "What is it going to take to get
it through your head that we are not related?"

"But—" How could he say that? They
were, too.

Whit read her thoughts before her befud-
dled mind could speak them. "It means
nothing that my father married your mother.
There's no blood tie between us. You aren't
my sister. You're a woman, and a damned
beautiful woman at that!"

A little shiver of sensual alarm ran down
her spine. She couldn't deal with this kind of
talk—not from Whit. She tried to push away
from him but he simply tightened his hold to
bring her closer to the bare wall of his chest.

Her hands were discovering a new sensation as they spread across the hard flesh of his shoulders in an attempt to keep some distance between them. His body heat seemed to burn them and the warmth radiated through her sensitive nerve ends.

"Whit, let me go." The breathless quality in her voice kept the request from being an order.

"If I were your brother, I wouldn't let you go." His hooded look roamed over her face. "I'd turn you over my knee for parading into a man's bedroom in that skimpy pair of frilly pajamas. But I'm not your brother so you'll get no spanking from me."

The glint in his eye warned her to expect an entirely different form of punishment. Until this moment, Shari hadn't believed he was capable of using physical force. Now, she was conscious of his sheer brute strength. She started trembling, even though part of her knew he wouldn't hurt her.

"I don't think you know what you're saying," she murmured in an effort to appeal to the reasonable side of his nature.

"I've been saying it for a long time, but you haven't been listening to me," Whit accused.

His arm circled her waist to hold her within its steel band while his fingers caught a handful of black hair in their grip. "You've been expecting too much from me, Shari. I'm a man—with the most human flaw of all—the desire for a woman. Is that what a brother would feel toward you?"

"No." She had to swallow to ease the tightness of her throat, a tightness that came from the intimate contact with his body.

Her legs felt weakened by the imprint of his thighs; muscled columns of male power. The wall of his naked chest loomed large, dwarfing her smaller frame. What little space separated her from it didn't lessen the potency of all that hard, tanned flesh. With each breath, she was drugged by the musky, male scent of his body.

"I can't pretend to be your brother anymore," he murmured and Shari found herself watching his mouth, unnerved by its masculine shape. "This charade had to end sometime."

She had just begun to realize it was moving closer when he eliminated the last inches to capture her lips. The safe, secure relationship she thought she and Whit had always possessed was shattered into a million pieces. She was in the arms of a stranger.

Initially, Shari was too stunned to resist the hungry plunder of his mouth. Then his mobile occupation of it left her too dazed by aroused sensations to consider it. The tantalizing probe of his hard tongue sent shivers of excitement licking through her veins. Whit breached her defenses with almost no effort.

Never in her wildest imagination would she have believed these earthy desires could burn with heat that seemed to melt her bones. Crazy, wild longings were building within her and she fought to keep them down.

With no need to subdue a resistance she wasn't offering, his hands began to wander over her shoulders, hips, and spine, restlessly exploring her curves and fitting her more fully to his length. The stimulation of their touch seemed to destroy what grip on reality she still maintained.

Her lips were suddenly cooled, exposed to the air when his mouth trailed across her cheek to the hollow below her ear. He caught the lobe of her ear between his teeth, nibbling at it with sensuous ease. Shari couldn't stop the shudder that quaked through her. His warm breath stirred her ear, starting more tremors.

"Would a brother make you feel like this?" Whit challenged huskily, revealing his awareness of the desires he was arousing within her.

"No." Her voice was hoarse, and she hated him for forcing her to admit that she was enjoying the sensations he was creating.

Shari discovered his hands had worked their way inside her robe. The looseness of her pajama top gave them easy access to her bare skin. The air was stripped from her lungs when his hand caught the fullness of a breast in its palm. The ache inside her was so intense that she wanted to cry out but she didn't have the strength.

"Would he touch you like this?" he demanded as he nuzzled her cheek, coming close to her lips yet resisting their parted invitation.

"No." Her answer verged on a whimper as her hands trembled over the flexed muscles of his shoulders.

Whit rubbed his mouth over her lips, enjoying their feel without taking them. "Would a brother be crazy to explore every inch of you?" His heated breath filled her mouth but this time he didn't wait for her admission. "I'm not your brother, Shari. I'm not going to let you pretend anymore that I am."

"Don't." She wasn't sure what she was protesting. His continual teasing of her lips or his determination to turn her into a quivering mass of desire.

"Do I have to take you to bed to convince you?" he demanded roughly.

There was a cold run of ice through her veins as she suddenly realized how easily that could happen. Seduction required a willing participant, and she had shown herself to be willing. To make matters worse, she was more than half-convinced Whit would be the ideal lover. She was instantly repelled by that incestuous thought.

Violently, she pushed away from him, holding the front of her robe closed with one hand and raising the back of her other hand to her mouth. She scrubbed it across her lips in an effort to erase the taste of him.

Her gaze studied him with a new perception. There was no attempt on his part to bridge the distance between them. His male virility was a very obvious thing to her now. Whit stood there, with his hands at his side, looking back at her. His bare chest rose and fell with the ragged tempo of his breathing.

Shari suddenly realized that this night could never be forgotten. They could never go back to the comfortable, secure relationship she'd known. Her stepbrother was lost to her forever. Her heart was twisted by the loss.

"Why did you do this?" she accused with a broken sob. "Why did you ruin everything?"

"Shari." Whit took a step toward her, his hand reaching out.

With a little cry, she pivoted away from him and ran to the door. Her shaking hand fumbled with the doorknob. For a panicked instant, she thought it was locked. Then she pulled it open and raced down the corridor to her room.

Whit was coming after her. Shari could hear the long strides of his footsteps. Breathing in sobs, she made it inside the room before he could catch up with her. She leaned against the door to keep him out and shakily turned the key in the lock.

The doorknob was rattled but it refused to turn. Her legs didn't seem to want to support her and Shari contiued to lean against the solidness of the door. Tears ran silently down her cheeks as she closed her eyes.

"Shari, let me in." His voice was pitched low and she knew he didn't want to waken the other sleeping members of the house.

"No, I won't." Her voice rasped out the refusal.

"Shari, please," Whit insisted in a fierce whisper, but she wouldn't answer him. She couldn't trust him—not anymore. She waited through the lengthy pause, knowing he hadn't left. "Are you all right?" he asked finally.

"No," she answered in a sobbing laugh. "I'm not all right." Shari closed her eyes tightly. "Go away. I don't know you."

"Yes, you do," he replied. "It's yourself you don't know."

With that, Shari heard him walk away. She didn't draw a breath until she heard the door to his room shut. She stumbled to the bed and threw herself across its length to cry silently for the friend and "brother" that had been taken from her.

IN THE past, it had often seemed that Whit was her only ally at Gold Leaf. Now Shari couldn't depend on him. She became withdrawn and quiet, almost as if she had gone into mourning. She associated with the Lancaster family only when the occasion demanded it, such as mealtimes. She took part in little of the conversations that went on, and ignored attempts by the elder Lancaster and Rory to include her.

Whit rarely spoke to her but his gaze seemed to be constantly on her. Any time he was in the same room with her, Shari was unsettled and on her guard. It seemed impossible to escape the tension. He electrified the air until it almost hurt to breathe.

Only with her mother did Shari find any kind of relief. She stayed long hours at the hospital with her. Even when she was released on Monday and came home, Shari rarely left her mother's side. A practical nurse, hired by Frederick Lancaster, took care of all Elizabeth's medical needs but it didn't matter to Shari that her presence wasn't needed every minute.

For more than a week, this continued. Once the routine was started, Shari didn't know how to break it, even if she wanted to change it. Which, she kept telling herself, she didn't. Whit's behavior had been unforgivable.

If she needed proof of that, she had it every night. She kept reliving that evening in her dreams. When she'd wake from them, Shari would remember everything in vivid detail. They disturbed her sleep to the point that rest was denied her. Each morning she awakened later and later.

The summer sun was blazing through her window when Shari dragged her tired eyes open and rolled over to look at the clock on her nightstand. She groaned at the time, the clock's hands showing it was going on nine. She was simply going to have to start setting the alarm, something she'd never had to do in her life.

Sitting up, Shari swung her legs over the side of the bed and paused in an attempt to clear her head of sleep's cobwebs. There was a knock at her door. She looked in its direction, comforted by the knowledge it was locked. It was always locked now.

"Yes?" Her voice was groggy with sleep. "Who is it?"

"It's me, Rory," came the cheerful reply. "Are you up?"

"Yes." In a manner of speaking she was, although she wouldn't describe herself as being alert.

When he tried the door and discovered it was locked, Shari pushed off the bed and grabbed her robe from the foot. Her legs carried her woodenly to the door while she shrugged into the robe and securely tied the front.

Rory knocked again. "Hey, Sis. Open up." He sounded puzzled.

With a turn of the key to unlock it, Shari pulled the door open. "What did you want?" She didn't bother with any preliminary greetings as she lifted the heavy weight of her hair away from her neck to rub the taut cords.

He was frowning. "How come you locked the door?"

To avoid his questioning eyes, her glance strayed past him. A thousand fire bells went off in her head when Shari found herself looking straight at Whit as he came out of his room. She stiffened, all her defenses bristling into life.

His dark gaze seemed to bore into her for a long second, hard and unyielding, yet he offered no greeting and didn't acknowledge her presence in any other manner. Rory turned to see what she was staring at just as Whit walked down the hall toward the stairs. His look was sharply curious when it returned to her.

Again, Shari couldn't meet her half brother's gaze and turned away from the door to seek refuge inside the room. It prodded her into remembering his question and she searched for an answer to discard his suspicions.

"I guess I got into the habit of locking it at college," she lied, unable to identify Whit as the cause.

"You've sure been acting strange lately," Rory declared. "You never used to sleep so late. I remember when you'd get me out of bed."

Shari didn't want to get into a conversation that analyzed her behavior. "What do you want?" She continued to keep her back on to him.

"I have an errand to run for Granddad, so I thought I'd see if there was anything you needed from town," he explained.

"I don't need anything," she replied shortly without turning around. "If that's all, would you please leave? I want to get dressed.''

"That's it, huh?" he challenged with exasperated patience. "No thanks for asking. Nothing. Just get out. I was trying to be kind and this is what I get for it."

Guiltily, Shari turned to face him. "I'm sorry," she apologized for her rudeness. "I guess I'm not awake."

"That's a convenient excuse." His expression revealed that he didn't believe her. "When we were growing up, I can't remember you and Whit ever quarreling. But when the two of you have a fight, it's a real dandy."

"I don't know what you're talking about." She paled at his statement. "What makes you think I've had a fight with Whit?"

"Aw, come on, Sis," Rory reproved her attempt to deny it. "It's as plain as the nose on your face. You don't speak to him; you go all stiff and cold every time you're in the same room together; and you've been walking around with a chip on your shoulder the size of a tree trunk. You're taking your anger out on everybody around you, except Mom. How long is this going to go on?"

"It doesn't concern you so just stay out of it." Shari didn't want to hear the things he was saying, but she couldn't seem to close her ears to them.

"How can I?" He lifted his hands, palms upward, in a helpless gesture. "I've got the feeling I'm caught in the middle of somebody else's war and I'm getting tired of being the innocent victim. I thought things would be better if you stayed, but you've got everyone walking around on tiptoes."

"It isn't like that at all," she protested impatiently.

"You wanta bet?" he challenged. "I don't know what started the argument the other night in Whit's room, but one of you has to make the first move. Why don't you just tell him you're sorry and end all this?"

Shari didn't hear anything he said past the mention of Whit's room. A chill ran down her spine. "How did you know I was in his room?" she asked in a stricken voice of alarm.

"I told you before that I can hear you guys talking," Rory reminded her. "I can't tell what you're saying, but I can hear your voices through the wall. I didn't realize you were fighting until you ran out of this room and I heard Whit come after you.''

A spasm of relief shook her. Shari didn't want Rory to know—she didn't want anyone to know what had transpired between herself and Whit. She didn't examine her reasons for that, not caring whether they came from a lingering sense of loyalty to the Whit Lancaster she had once known or the guilt of her own initial, and not unwilling, role in the scene.

"What *did* you argue about?" Rory frowned. "It couldn't have been about you going back to Duke University. That was already settled."

"It's none of your business," Shari answered sharply.

A heavy sigh came from him. "At least you and Whit say the same thing."

"You mean you asked him about it?" Shari wanted to be sure she understood him correctly.

"Yes, but he was just as closemouthed about the whole thing as you are," Rory complained.

"Then why don't you take the hint and stay out of it?" she suggested. "It's none of your affair anyway."

"I'm only trying to help," he insisted in his own defense.

"Instead of being so concerned about the personal differences between Whit and me, you'd better concentrate on solving your own problems," she said, finding a way to end the conversation. "Instead of standing here talking to me, you should be on your way to town to take care of that errand for Granddad. If you don't, you're going to be in trouble with him."

"Running errands is all anybody thinks I'm good for around this place," Rory griped. "Nobody listens to me. They just pat me on the head and tell me to be a good boy and run along."

Shari realized that she hadn't been very understanding. As he turned to leave, she added, "Thanks for caring, Rory."

He paused to look back and slanted her a half-smile. "I'm just your kid brother. What do I know about anything?" he mocked without any bitterness and walked into the hall, closing the door behind him.

Alone in her room once again, Shari was reminded again of the lateness of the hour by the bright sunlight pouring into the room. The summer day already promised to be a hot one.

The thick walls of the old southern mansion kept out a lot of the heat, but it still needed the assistance of central air conditioning to keep the temperature inside at a comfortable level. Shari dressed for the season in a pair of blue cotton slacks and a lighter blue T-shirt with the insignia of her sorority printed on the front.

Before going downstairs for a late breakfast, she stopped in her mother's room. Elizabeth Lancaster was seated in one of the cushioned chairs in the sitting area of her large bedroom, listening to the radio. Shari smiled at the sight of her mother up and about after seeing her so many times in bed.

"Good-morning." She walked over to kiss her mother's cheek.

"Good-morning, sleepyhead." Her mother still spoke slowly but with much less effort. "I was beginning to wonder where you were."

"I just got up," Shari admitted. "Need I ask how you are this morning?"

"If I told you I'm going to ask the doctor to let me come downstairs and have dinner with the family tonight, would that answer your question?" she countered with a small smile.

"Yes, I think it would. When's Doctor Franck coming? This afternoon?" she asked.

"Yes, he's supposed to be here around two, barring any emergencies," her mother explained, then her maternal instincts surfaced. "Have you had breakfast yet?"

"No, I was just going downstairs, and decided to check on you first." Shari didn't wait to be lectured on the necessity of starting out the day with a nourishing breakfast. "Would you like me to bring a book from the library when I come back?"

"Yes." Her mother nodded with a twinkle in her eyes. "Make it a murder mystery."

"I'll pick out one with bodies lying all over the place," Shari laughed.

"Please, not too many," she admonished with a faint smile. "Now, go eat your breakfast."

The downstairs seemed empty. There wasn't a soul around, although Shari heard the steady hum of a vacuum cleaner coming

from one of the rooms. She didn't disturb
Mrs. Youngblood from her morning cleaning
and bypassed the dining room. The table had
already been cleared of breakfast dishes.

She went straight to the kitchen to fix her
own small breakfast. There was coffee in the
pot. Shari poured herself a cup, got a glass of
orange juice from the refrigerator, and fixed
two slices of toast. It was too close to lunchtime to have a full morning meal.

When she had finished, Shari washed up
her own dishes and put them away in the cupboards. She left the kitchen to go to the library crossing her fingers that she wouldn't
run into Whit.

CHAPTER SEVEN

WHEN SHARI neared the library, the sound of the vacuum cleaner grew louder. At the doorway, she saw the housekeeper running the machine over the large area rug. Shari hesitated to enter, not wanting to get in the woman's way, but Mrs. Youngblood saw her and motioned her into the room.

For the most part, the library was the domain of the Lancaster males. As a result, its decor was very masculine. There was a preponderance of darkly stained wood, heavy furniture covered in burgundy-red leather, and a massive, centuries-old desk and chair.

The housekeeper made one more swipe across the print rug as Shari entered the library, then switched off the vacuum cleaner. Aware that her grandfather constantly shooed Mrs. Youngblood out of the library before she could finish her cleaning, Shari didn't want the woman to feel she had to stop because she was there.

"Don't let me interrupt you," she protested. "I'm just going to get a book for Mother and I'll be gone."

"You're not," Mrs. Youngblood insisted. "Miracle of miracles, I'm through. The minute Mr. Frederick went out for a walk, I dashed in here. For once, I have it all cleaned before he returned."

Shari smiled in silent understanding. "I didn't want you to think I was chasing you out."

She mentally filed away the information that her grandfather was taking a morning stroll, but she didn't ask where Whit was. She presumed he was also outside somewhere.

"You missed breakfast," the housekeeper said as she unplugged the vacuum cleaner cord and began winding it up. "Would you like me to fix you something?"

"I've already raided the kitchen," Shari admitted and walked to the bookshelves that filled the wall next to the brick fireplace. "I think I can make it until lunch."

The housekeeper rolled the silent vacuum cleaner toward the doorway. "The library is all yours. Would you answer the phone if it rings? I can't always hear it when I'm cleaning," she explained.

"Of course," Shari promised.

A few minutes later, the vacuum cleaner was started up again, its loud hum coming from the living room. Shari paid little attention to it, busy perusing the fiction titles in search of a novel her mother might enjoy.

Just as she took an Agatha Christie book from the shelf to glance through, she thought she heard footsteps. She turned her head to absently glance toward the door. Her heart and lungs seemed to stop functioning. Whit was halfway into the library before he noticed her standing by the bookshelves. He stopped abruptly.

Her fingers tightened around the hardbound book, all her senses sharpened by his presence. The story line of the novel ceased to be important. The only thing that mattered now was getting out of the room. Her pulse was running away with itself, sending a heat coursing through her veins.

The tension in the air was so intense it seemed suffocating. With the book clutched tightly in her hand, Shari tore her gaze from

Whit's strong features and started for the door.

"Don't go yet," he stated. "I want to talk to you."

Shari faltered for an instant, almost responding to the firm authority in his voice. She caught herself in time.

"We have nothing to say to each other." She was deliberately cold.

With her head held high, Shari walked to the opened door. She had almost reached the safety of the entry hall when Whit grabbed her arm and pulled her back into the library, closing the door to shut them both in. Shari had been trying so hard to avoid a situation like this where she was alone with him. She was rigid with a panic she didn't want him to see.

"I said I wanted to talk to you," Whit repeated.

Shari was reminded that his word was always accompanied by action. He didn't believe in arguing a point. He intended to talk to her whether or not she wanted to listen. In a show of stubbornness, she clamped her mouth shut, intending for it to be a strictly one-sided conversation.

The set of his jaw was hard with displeasure when he studied her defiant expression. Her attitude was plain and Whit was able to read her like a book. His gaze narrowed in grim disapproval.

"How long do you intend to carry on this war of silence?" Whit challenged.

Shari refused to answer him. It was useless to try for the door. Whit would only catch her and haul her back, so she turned into the room. But he caught her arm again to swing her around and force Shari to face him.

This time his hold on her arm brought a vivid rush of memories. She couldn't be indifferent to it or them. Alone in the library with him, there was too much chance that the scene in his bedroom might be repeated.

"Don't touch me," she warned, her teeth tightly clenched to keep the tremor out of her voice.

Whit breathed out a silent, humorless laugh and didn't let her go. "It's no good telling me that—not after I've held you and kissed you. I couldn't stay away from you any more than a drowning man can stop himself from grabbing at a rope."

A little shiver trickled down her spine, because Shari knew he was right. They had crossed a bridge, and there wasn't any going back. Struggling against the grip of his hand could incite him into something more physical, so Shari chose to stiffly stand her ground in silent resistance. But her senses were reacting to him, disturbed in a way that was more sensual than scared. She had to resist them as well.

"Do you think I wanted this to happen?" Whit demanded. "I tried to deny what I was feeling for you but I couldn't. And I can't."

She lowered her gaze to the front of his shirt; the material was stretched across his flatly muscled chest, pulling at the buttons. It was extremely easy to recall the feel of the hard flesh the shirt concealed, and the sensations touching it had aroused.

"That's your problem," Shari insisted because she had her hands full with her own.

"I've waited a long time for you to look at me as a man," he stated. "You did the other night, for the first time."

Holding her silence, Shari didn't bother to correct him that it hadn't been the first time. She'd had glimpses of him a few times just prior to that night, because of things Doré had said and the territorial instincts that had surfaced. But she wasn't any better prepared for such recognition now than she was then.

"You know I'm right. Why won't you admit it?" Whit showed some of his impatience with her.

"I'll admit nothing because there's nothing to admit!" Shari lied vigorously. "I hate you for the way you've ruined everything."

"What did I ruin?" He shook his head in a kind of quiet disgust. "I was never your brother. You chose to look upon me as one, but that's not what I was. That's not what I am."

"Don't you see?" she argued. "I can never trust you again. It will never be the same between us!"

"If you gave it a chance, it would be better," he insisted.

"No!" She wouldn't even consider that possibility.

"Shall I prove it?" Whit challenged with an arching brow that seemed to mock her denial.

"Leave me alone. That's all I want from you." Shari strained away from him, not trying to break free yet wanting as much distance between them as possible. A treacherous temptation was insidiously working on her system in the face of his suggestive challenge. "If it hadn't been for Mother, I would have left this house the next morning and never come back."

"Your mother wasn't the only reason you stayed." He smoothly dismissed her explanation. "There's a part of you that felt something happen that night. Curiosity made you stay to see if it could happen again."

"That's not true." But a quiver of apprehension removed the conviction from her voice, because that traitorous curiosity was working on her right now.

She was conscious of his masculine build, the understated potency of his male charm, and the unnerving line of his mouth. In spite of her determination to show indifference, Shari was stimulated by his closeness, the familiar aroma of tobacco that clung to his clothes and mingled with his own individual scent, and the clean, strong lines of his features.

"Prove it, then," Whit challenged.

"How?" She was thrown into confusion.

"Kiss me the way you would kiss Rory." He eyed her with a knowing look that openly doubted her ability to do it.

"That's ridiculous," Shari protested with ill-concealed panic. "Why should I have to prove anything to you?"

"You're not proving it to me," he countered. "You're proving it to yourself."

"And the result would be your interpretation." She was thinking fast, trying to find a way out of the dangerous entrapment of his challenge. "If I kissed you the same way I would kiss Rory, there would be warmth and love in it. You'd simply take that and twist it into something entirely different."

"Like desire, for instance?" Whit mocked her softly, and Shari trembled a little because she could feel that sensation stirring inside her.

When he took the book out of her hand, there didn't seem to be anything she could do about it. She felt helpless and she hated the feeling. Resisting Whit was like crossing swords with a master fencer. She'd never win.

But Shari wasn't a quitter. Defiance shimmered in her green eyes as he slowly pulled her rigid body into his arms, but they closed when his mouth settled onto hers. At first, its pressure tantalized her lips, almost laughing at their rigid line. The pervasive warmth of his embrace spread through her limbs while he slowly deepened the kiss.

At some point, she began kissing him back, returning the lazy ardor. The circle of his arms tightened to mold her to his hard length. The instant Shari realized how quickly she had surrendered, she turned her head away from him and tightly closed her eyes in self-reproach.

"There's nothing sinful about wanting me, Shari," he murmured near her ear. The gentle insistence of his tone almost persuaded her to believe him. "It's as natural as breathing."

"I can't," she protested in a husky voice. "Not after all these years."

"I know you need time to adjust," Whit admitted grudgingly and lifted his head. "That's why I've stayed away from you this past week so you could think things through for yourself."

When Shari pushed out of his arms, Whit didn't try to stop her. "I want you to stay away from me," she insisted, because she knew that she couldn't trust herself anymore.

"I won't," he warned. "You're rejecting me for the wrong reasons."

"How can you be so sure?" She was forced into defying him. "You think you know everything! Well, you don't!"

"I don't know everything, but I know you," Whit stated with calm certainty.

Shari sought refuge in a general anger at his sex. "I'm wasting my time talking to you. You Lancasters are all alike. Your opinion is the only one that matters." Agitated, she looked around. "Where did you put the book I had? I was taking it to Mother."

"It's right here." He picked it up from a side table and handed it to her, faint amusement showing through his arrogant expression. That only angered her more.

Jerking the book out of his hand, Shari held onto it tightly and searched desperately for something suitably cutting to say. She didn't have time to find it as the library door was opened behind her, and the elder Lancaster hobbled in with his cane. She looked back when he stopped and eyed the two of them, his aging features wearing an expression of warm satisfaction.

"The two of you are on speaking terms again," he remarked. "It's about time. No good comes from brothers and sisters fighting."

"Whit isn't my brother," Shari stated with faint sarcasm. "Don't take my word for it. Ask him." She tossed the challenge over her shoulder, daring Whit to bring the issue out into the open.

"I'm not her brother," he admitted it readily, then went a step further. "You might as well get used to the idea, Granddad, because I'm going to marry her."

Shari went white with shock, then erupted into a full-blown anger. "Over my dead body!"

"You will be very much alive on our wedding night!" Whit snapped, answering her with equal force. "That, I promise you!"

"You're crazy." She was trembling. "I'll never marry you."

"Yes, you will." The absolute certainty of his steady gaze was unnerving. "You'll marry me and you'll like it."

Her glance swung to the elder man, leaning heavily on his cane. He was watching their exchange with what appeared to be enjoyment. Any thought that he might come to her aid was immediately dashed.

"He's crazy, Granddad," Shari appealed to him anyway.

"I think he's making a lot of sense," he replied blandly. "I don't know of any other man who could handle you except Whit."

"I don't *need* anyone to handle me!" she flared. "I can take care of myself."

"Every woman should have a man to take care of her," Frederick Lancaster insisted.

"That attitude went out of style with shoulder pads!" Shari declared in disgust. "It's only you Lancaster men that are holdouts."

"I have no intention of taking care of you," Whit informed her. "In fact, I plan on it being the other way around. But you can't disagree that every woman should have a man to love her."

"No, I don't disagree with that," she retorted. "But I don't want you to be the one who loves me."

"There isn't anything you can do about it, so you might as well accept it," he stated.

She turned on Frederick Lancaster in a temper, her green eyes glazing. "This is all your fault!'' she accused. ''You're always trying to make decision for other people. Whit is following in your footsteps. You're wrong—both of you!''

There wasn't a better exit line, so Shari used that one to storm out of the library. She nearly ran over the housekeeper busy dusting the furniture in the entry hall.

''Here.'' Shari stopped and shoved the book into Mrs. Youngblood's hands. ''Would you take this upstairs to my mother and tell her I'm going for a walk. I'll see her around lunchtime.''

Taking it for granted that the housekeeper would do as she asked, Shari didn't wait for a reply. She swept out of the house and down the front steps of the portico, not slowing down until she was well away from the house.

The slower pace was not the result of a cooling temper. It was dictated by the heat of a summer sun, beating down on the earth. Perspiration was collecting under the heavy weight of the hair on her neck. She lifted it so the drifting breeze could reach it as she strolled past the bulk barns.

They were another example of the changes at Gold Leaf. Nothing was as it had been, not

Whit and not the processing of the money crop—tobacco. When Shari was a child, the old gold leaves of tobacco had been painstakingly tied to sticks, then racked on poles to be cured in the old log tobacco barns.

She missed the old, twin-eaved structures. It didn't matter how labor-efficient the bulk barns were. Leaves, the size of a blade from a huge ceiling fan, were stacked in the barns for curing, a much simpler system.

But it somehow lacked the romance of the first—just as Whit's announcement that they were going to be married had lacked the flourishes and frills. Shari simmered with indignation at his high-handed manner—and Granddad Lancaster's endorsement of Whit's decision. Neither cared what she thought or felt. She might as well have been a child for all the notice they took of her opinion.

Somewhere along the line, Shari had begun to accept the concept that Whit was not her brother, and never had been—perhaps because of the elder Lancaster's easy acceptance of it. She was also becoming reconciled to the physical attraction she felt toward Whit. But she would never accept someone telling her what she would do.

Marriage had never been mentioned by Whit. He hadn't even proposed to her. And he'd never said that he loved her. He had simply informed her they were going to be married and she was going to like the idea. Just thinking about the arrogance of it all made her blood boil.

The Lancasters weren't the only ones who had pride. Shari possessed it in abundance, too. No one had ever ruled her, although Frederick Lancaster had tried. She was determined that Whit Lancaster would fare no better.

She paused at the stables where the carriage horses and hunters had once been housed during that long ago era of Gold Leaf. Only three horses were stabled there now. The fat, white gelding called Snowdance had been Rory's first horse.

The gentle old beast had been retired to the pasture years ago. Rory had sentimentally refused to sell the gelding, afraid it would wind up in a glue factory. Now it was living out its years in the company of two young, spirited steeds.

The black horse was a recent present to Rory from his grandfather, a coming six year old, but Rory hadn't taken much interest in Coaldust. Shari suspected he had outgrown his horse phase. The golden chestnut approached the paddock fence at a gliding trot, its flaxen mane and tail flaring out like a banner. Banner was the four year old's name.

Shari admired the classy horse as it came to the fence rail where she was standing and curiously thrust its velvet nose toward her. Banner belonged to Whit. There was a boldness about the horse that seemed to match its owner, spirited without being high-strung or nervous.

As Shari stroked its sleek neck, the horse nuzzled the front of her T-shirt, trying to find the pockets that usually contained pieces of carrot or apple. With a laugh, she pushed its nose away. It faded into a smile as Shari recalled the many times she had gone horseback riding with Whit.

Her own horse had been a feisty gray gelding that she had named Rebel, but Shari had sold him when she'd entered college. She wished she had him back. Together they had wildly ridden off a lot of her anger, tearing across the fields and racing the wind until her temper had cooled.

It was nearly noon before she retraced her path to the house. Shari felt relatively calm, all things considered, as she entered the air-cooled house. From the dining room, there was the muted clatter of the table being set for lunch.

The library door was closed when she passed it. Shari glanced at it, an emerald sparkle of defiance in her eyes. She paused in the dining room to see if Mrs. Youngblood needed any help with lunch, expecting and receiving the refusal. Then, she continued on to the ground floor washroom to clean up before lunch.

A few minutes later, she returned to the dining room. Frederick Lancaster was already seated at the head of the table. Whit and Rory were just taking their seats. Whit paused to pull out the chair beside his for Shari, but she walked around the table to sit next to Rory. The amber glint in his dark eyes seemed to accept the veiled challenge of her gesture and silently warned her it wouldn't go unanswered.

"Boy, Sis, you are a dark one," Rory declared with a grinning smile.

Her gaze darted across the table to Whit, a whisper of alarm in her head. But Whit didn't appear to be paying any attention to her. A dark vitality was evident in his smoothly hewn features. Shari was positive he had something to do with Rory's remarks. The thought was reinforced by the suggestion of a complacent smile deepening the corners of his mouth.

"Why do you say that?" There was wary caution in the question she put to Rory. She had to be sure what he meant by his remark.

"Because of your engagement to Whit," he replied as if it were obvious. "I still don't understand why the two of you were so secretive about the way you felt toward each other. You aren't actually related."

For a count of ten, Shari kept her lips lying flatly against each other and looked across the table at the I-told-you-so glitter in Whit's eyes. She was determined not to lose her temper, not this time. It had gained her nothing during their encounter in the library.

"I'm sure glad—" Rory went on, "—that the two of you have finally made up after your lover's quarrel. Things can get back to normal around here now."

"I doubt if things will get back to normal, Rory," Shari said smoothly and with smiling calm. "You have been misinformed. There wasn't any lover's quarrel. And there isn't any engagement."

Her young brother's mouth opened and closed for a confused second as he glanced from her to Whit. "But... Whit said...."

"Whit is a Lancaster," she pointed out in what sounded like a reasonable tone. "He thinks he has the final word on everything. But he's wrong."

Rory was confused. "Aren't you going to marry him?"

"No."

"Yes."

Both Shari and Whit answered simultaneously, their replies cancelling each other out. Their glances locked across the table. Shari's was cool and challenging, although inside she was simmering. Whit's dark eyes revealed easy confidence, and a hint of amusement at her denial.

With a bewildered shake of his head, Rory looked at his plate. "I wish I knew what was going on here."

"Shari is simply trying to establish her independence," Whit explained. "She's afraid of losing it if she becomes Mrs. Whit Lancaster."

"I have no intention of losing it—or allowing you to run my life," she bristled at his accusation. She was afraid, but she suspected it was another one of his tricks. She wasn't about to play into his hand when she didn't have the trump card.

Whit deliberately ignored her response and addressed himself to Rory. "It'll take her some time to get used to the idea of being my wife. But she'll come around."

The very sound of his voice was possessive and the way his dark glance ran over her was equally so. Referring to her as his wife carried a connotation of marital intimacy that Shari suddenly couldn't handle. The thought of lying naked in his arms filled her with a coursing heat that scorched her raw nerve ends. Too many remembered and imagined sensations went spinning through her mind.

"I'm not going to marry you, Whit." Shari had to deny him to regain control of her nearly shattered composure, but she lacked the strength to meet his gaze. She tried to assume an air of calm indifference. "You are just making a fool of yourself by saying that I will."

"We'll see," he murmured with an apparent lack of concern. "Would you pass me the salt?"

His confidence was infuriating, especially when her own was a little shaky. Shari longed to hurl the saltshaker at him and run from the room. Such an action would be an admission that her objections were being worn down. Shari was determined to remain at the table and swallow every bite of lunch even if she choked on it. Whit appeared to know that, which didn't help the situation at all.

No further reference was made to the supposed engagement during the rest of the noon meal. When lunch was finished, Shari helped the housekeeper clear the dishes from the table while the men excused themselves.

The fine tension that claimed her didn't go away when Whit left the house to finish his day's work. It remained to thread through her veins, never letting the thought of him stray far.

She was struggling with it when she climbed the stairs to spend the afternoon with her mother. The middle-aged practical nurse was on her way down the steps, carrying the lunch tray Mrs. Youngblood had sent up.

"Did Mother eat well?" Shari asked, because she was often guilty of picking at her food.

"She cleaned up every bit of it," Nurse Jeffers informed her with a wide smile. "May I offer you my congratulations on your engagement to Mr. Lancaster?"

Shari stiffened to a halt halfway up the stairs. The news had spread fast. She realized that was natural at Gold Leaf, especially when there was a Lancaster involved.

"I'm not engaged to Whit," she flatly denied it, intending to crush the rumor before it went any further. "I'm not engaged to anyone. Whoever told you otherwise was lying."

The nurse's mouth dropped open, but Shari didn't wait to hear any apology or explanation. She climbed the rest of the stairs with quick impatient steps; their sound was a rapid tattoo that told of her barely contained temper.

Outside her mother's door, Shari paused to take a deep breath and fix a bright expression on her face. When she walked in, her mother was lying in bed, propped in a sitting position by pillows. Shari recognized the book her mother was holding as the one she had selected from the library that morning.

"Is it good?" she asked, drawing her mother's glance.

"Shari!" Her mother said with some surprise. "I didn't expect to see you this afternoon."

"Why not?" She laughed shortly in confusion.

"I presumed you would go into town with Whit to pick out your engagement ring," she explained and closed the novel to set it aside.

Shock drained the color from her face. Shari hadn't dreamed that the news had spread all the way to her mother's room.

"Who told you such a thing?" She wanted to know the identity of the informant, guessing it was either the nurse or the housekeeper. All the while she struggled to contain her irritation and hide it from her mother.

A slight frown creased her mother's face as she tried to recall. "I don't think it was actually said that you would accompany Whit, but it seemed logical that you would."

Shari wasn't interested in the business about the ring. She shook her head to dismiss that subject. "I mean, who told you about the engagement?"

Her mother's smile was vaguely bewildered. "Why, Whit did, of course." And Shari wanted to scream her frustration. To make matters worse, her mother misinterpreted the agitation in Shari's attitude. "I couldn't have been happier when he told me the two of you were going to be married."

"He shouldn't have told you that." Shari tried to calmly correct the information.

"I quite understand that you would have preferred to be with him when he told me but I think Whit wanted to do it all properly by talking to me first in private."

"He shouldn't have told you because the announcement was premature," Shari went one step further in her statement. "I haven't agreed to marry him."

"You needn't withhold your answer because of me," her mother replied, still not recognizing what Shari was trying to tell her. "I am really so much better that there isn't any reason to postpone your engagement to him."

"You're not listening to me, Mom." She continued to speak calmly, stretching her patience to the limit. "I have not agreed to marry Whit."

Her frown deepened. "But this morning, he said—"

"He was speaking out of turn," Shari interrupted with a forceful assertion.

But she could tell her mother still didn't believe her. Shari suddenly realized why. A man had told her—a Lancaster man, and Elizabeth Lancaster accepted their word without question. It was her nature. She wouldn't believe otherwise until Whit said it was so. Shari was so frustrated she wanted to take her mother by the shoulders and shake some sense into her.

She clamped down on the impulse. In her mother's physical condition, just recovering from a stroke, Shari didn't want to risk upsetting her by arguing. She would simply have to find another way to deal with the problem.

It seemed safer to change the subject. "What time did you say the doctor was coming?"

"This afternoon, around two," her mother explained.

"Would you do me a favor and not say anything to him about Whit and me?" Shari requested with a strained smile. "I don't want anyone else to know."

"Naturally you want a little time to yourselves." Her mother made her own interpretation of the request. Shari didn't waste her breath trying to deny it.

An hour later, the doctor arrived. Shari stepped out of the room while he conducted his examination of her mother. She went downstairs and directly to the library. Granddad Lancaster was the only one in the room.

"Did you want to see me?" He looked up in sharp inquiry when she entered the library without knocking—a definite breach of Lancaster etiquette.

"I was looking for Whit," she stated.

"I'm afraid he's out. I don't expect him back until dinnertime," he said.

"I want to see him the minute he comes back," Shari said and emphasized it by repeating it. "The very minute he comes back. You tell him that."

She was determined to have him correct this intolerable situation with her mother. She didn't want her to continue to believe they were engaged.

"I'll tell him," Granddad Lancaster promised.

CHAPTER EIGHT

THERE WAS a blue-black sheen to her freshly washed hair as Shari styled it with the blow dryer. She had stepped out of the shower not fifteen minutes earlier. For the fourth time, she had to stop to retuck the end of the bath towel wrapped around her. It would have been simpler to put on a robe but it seemed pointless to get the one in her bedroom now. She was nearly finished.

Her wristwatch was lying on the marble-topped counter by the sink. She glanced at the time it indicated—a few minutes before five o'clock—and tried to speculate what time Whit would arrive home.

Her temper simmered every time she thought about him informing her mother of their supposed engagement. Did he think that by telling everybody she would begin to accept it as an accomplished fact? If he did, he had another think coming.

Viewing her reflection in the bathroom mirror, Shari was satisfied with the way her hair looked and switched off the dryer. The makeup could be applied later, after she had dressed for the evening meal.

It was going to be a special occasion, since the doctor had given her mother permission to join the family downstairs. That was the biggest reason Shari wanted this absurd matter of her engagement cleared up before then. She didn't want it to be a topic of conversation at dinner tonight.

As she left the private bath adjoining her bedroom, Shari started to loosen the tucked corner of the towel so she could immediately dress in the clothes already laid out on her bed. She stopped short when she saw Whit standing a step inside her room, and recovered just in time to catch the towel before it could slip out of position.

"What are you doing in here?" she accused.

"I knocked and called your name but you evidently didn't hear me." His traveling glance was inspecting her from head to toe, taking special note of her bare limbs.

There was something almost physical about the way he looked at her. Her reaction to it was very definitely physical, her pulse stimulated to a faster tempo, and a warmth spreading over her skin.

"And you walked in just the same." Shari tried to secure the towel without making a project out of it, feigning an indifference she was far from feeling.

But her action attracted his glance to her breasts as the towel stretched tautly across them. Shari was reluctant to draw a breath or allow any movement that might increase his interest.

"I thought I heard a noise," Whit explained and slowly lifted his glance to her face. There was a faint curve to his mouth when he observed the heightened color in her cheeks. "I decided to check to see if you were here since you made such an issue of seeing me before dinner."

"Yes, I did." Shari allowed herself to be sidetracked. "You are going to speak to my mother and clear up this impression she has that you and I are engaged."

"But we are," he insisted in a perfectly reasonable voice.

"We are not!" she retorted.

Whit just smiled and reached into the side pocket of his light tan suit jacket. When his hand came out, he was holding a small, square box.

"This is for you," he said and tossed it to her, not crossing the short distance to actually hand it to her.

Shari reached for it and missed. It landed on the floor near her bare feet. She stooped down to pick it up, recognizing it instantly as a ring box.

"What is this?" she challenged.

"Your engagement ring," Whit replied smoothly.

She didn't know whether she was more angered by his presumption that she would wear it or the casual way he'd given it to her—almost indifferent. Her fingers tightened around the corners of the box, wishing it was his jugular vein.

"Is this a peculiar custom of the Lancasters?" Shari questioned with a trace of sarcasm. "Throwing engagement rings at girls?"

His low chuckle was throaty and amused. "If I got down on one knee to you, you'd kick me in the teeth—and we both know it," he mocked.

"You're right. I probably would." She was nearly angry enough to at least try it.

"Aren't you going to open the box and look at the ring?" Whit prompted.

Shari hesitated for an instant, almost tempted. "No," she refused. "I don't want it." She tossed it back to him, and Whit caught it with a one-handed grab. "I guess you'll have to take it back. You were a fool to buy it in the first place."

"No." He rolled the box around between his fingers for a few seconds, then set it on top of an oak chest of drawers. "I'm not going to take it back. It's yours."

"I'll just throw it away," she warned him.

"If you do, I'll buy you another one." He wasn't the least put off by her threat.

Sheer frustration ran through her. "Why don't you listen to me?" she protested. "There isn't any engagement! And there isn't going to be any marriage!"

Whit studied her without saying anything. Shari pivoted, turning her back to him and silently damning him for being so immovable. How many times in the past had she known him to take a firm stand and refuse to be moved? Too many.

"Whit Lancaster, you just can't have everything your own way," she insisted tightly.

"I haven't." His voice seemed closer, and she realized he must have come up behind her. "The problem is you have had your way for too long. Everyone has always given in to what you want—including me. You wanted me to be your big brother—and I tried to be what you wanted." When he paused, Shari felt his hand slide under her hair and curve itself to the back of her neck. Her skin seemed to come alive under his touch. "I can't pretend anymore that I don't want you in the way that a man wants a woman."

His words, his voice, his touch were kindling little fires inside her; wildfires that could burn out of control if she let him continue.

"Please let me go?" Shari tried to make it sound like a very reasonable request, concealing any hint that she was disturbed by him.

"No, that isn't what you want me to do." His hand moved from the base of her neck into her shoulder while his other hand took a position on the opposite side. They moved with restless interest over the bareness of her shoulders and down her arms. "I haven't figured out why you won't admit it."

When his fingers slid off her arms to cross her stomach, Shari was gently molded against the hard outline of his body. She closed her eyes, fighting the heady sensation it caused.

"You are very experienced in the way of making a woman feel things." She offered it as a justification for her own aroused state.

"Is that what's bothering you?" he asked, and his mouth moved against her hair. "Because I know how to give you pleasure, yet you don't know how to please me. I'll gladly teach you. We can have the first lesson now."

When his hands cupped her breasts, the towel covering them seemed ineffectual. The sensation of possession burned right through the material and Shari stiffened.

Whit nuzzled the lobe of her ear, his warm breath stirring up excitement in the shell-like opening. "Don't fight what you're feeling. Enjoy it."

She turned her head to the side in what was intended to be the beginning of a negative movement, but it lacked any follow-through. A sensual heat was weakening her defenses.

"Don't *tell* me I have to enjoy it." Didn't he understand the issue here? She wouldn't be told what to do, who to marry, or who to love.

"Then make me enjoy it," Whit challenged and turned her around.

His mouth hovered close to her lips, waiting for her to take up his invitation. A little thrill of power ran through her as she let her gaze wander over his handsomely carved features bent so closely to her.

Her fingertips traced the clean line of his jaw all the way to the prominent bone in his cheek. Then Shari let her fingers succumb to the urge to bury themselves in the vital thickness of his hair. They applied pressure to bring his mouth the last little distance to hers.

The aggressive side of her nature had always been forced to stay in the background, never showing itself when she was in a man's arms—until now. It added a volatile dimension to the embrace, setting both of them on fire.

She was crushed against his body by his circling arms, the material of his pants rough against the bareness of her thighs. His mouth mated with hers, the completeness of that union leaving them hungry for something more.

The world seemed to spin at a crazy speed, but the ride was deliciously exhilarating.

When he scooped her up into the cradle of his arms, the towel was pulled loose, but the closeness of their bodies held it in place. Shari trembled with utter pleasure at the dark desire blazing in his eyes as he scanned the rapt expression on her features.

"Do you see the way it will be after we're married?" His voice was husky and rough, disturbed by the rapid pattern of his breathing.

Looking at him now, Shari wondered how she could ever have seen him in a brotherly light. He was much too virile and earthy, too sexually exciting. Perhaps, regarding him as a big brother had been a defense mechanism of her heart to keep her from falling hopelessly in love with him.

It was useless to speculate about that now, but one thing was certain. "I bet you'd really be the ideal lover," she whispered.

She was conscious of his chest swelling on a quickly indrawn breath that was slow to be released. He carried her to the bed as if she weighed no more than a tied bundle of tobacco leaves on which the family fortune was founded.

As he laid her down, Whit left room on the edge of the mattress so he could sit facing her. The covering towel had slid down around her waist and hips, but Shari couldn't remember why she needed to cover herself. In fact, there was a certain pride in knowing that he liked what he saw.

"This isn't a passing thing for you or me," Whit said and let his hand travel slowly up her neck to caress the smooth line of her jaw. "We'll feel like this when our grandchildren are playing on the front lawn."

"First, there have to be children before there can be grandchildren," she reminded him with a faint smile.

His gaze lingered on the full shape of her lips, softly swollen from his kisses. His thumb moved over to trace their outline, then gently forced them apart. Her teeth, lightly and sensuously, nibbled on the calloused, rounded point of his thumb, the tip of her tongue tasting the salty flavor of his skin with its tang of nicotine.

The line of his mouth took on a certain dry humor. "I hope I bother you as much as you bother me,'' he murmured and drew his hand away.

Her laugh was soft and a little throaty, quietly reveling in the power she was just learning she had over him. For the time being, Shari didn't dwell on the knowledge that Whit possessed an equal power over her. That she had known, but hers was a new experience.

When she shifted to make more room for him, she caught a glimpse of white polka dots on a background of ocean-green silk beneath her. She was lying on the clothes she'd set out to wear that evening—with a damp towel beneath her to compound the problem. Shari reacted with dismay.

''My clothes!'' She pushed at Whit to get him off the bed and scrambled after him when he did, dragging the towel with her.

The instant she was on her feet, she turned to survey the damage. The dampness of the towel had virtually ironed the wrinkles into her clothes.

''I was going to wear that to dinner tonight,'' she complained to Whit.

The gold lights in his eyes were dancing with laughter while the deepened corners of his mouth held in a smile. ''Do you suppose this is the way it will be after we're married, too?'' he asked with definite amusement. ''From now on, don't put clothes on the bed. Keep them in the closet.''

''And what am I supposed to do about tonight?'' Shari challenged, because it wasn't that humorous to her.

''I'd be very happy if you came as you are,'' Whit murmured with a lazy, raking glance at her nude form only fractionally hidden from him by the towel absently clutched in her hand. ''Unfortunately, it would probably raise a few eyebrows.

A degree of inhibition returned. Shari suddenly wasn't as comfortable as she had been with his eyes seeing so much of her. Her hand lifted the towel to the valley between her breasts to at least conceal the frontal view from him.

''You aren't very helpful,'' she replied.

His gaze flicked to the towel. ''It's a little late for that.''

''That's your opinion.'' Shari lifted a bare shoulder to indicate indifference but it was a faked gesture. She wasn't indifferent at all.

When he gathered her into his arms, it was as if he was dealing with a reluctant child.

There was amused indulgence in his look, and a patient curve to his mouth. Only his hands gave away that he knew he was holding a woman.

They roamed idly over the bareness of her lower spine and hips, their touch pleasantly rough against the silken smoothness of her skin. Shari kept the towel between them, firmly holding onto it.

"You have to leave, Whit." If she let him continue, they'd be back on the bed. "I need to get dressed."

"It's a shame to hide such a beautiful body," he murmured, running his hands over it. There was a wry slant to his mouth after he'd spoken. "But I don't want anyone to see it except me."

Bending his head, he rolled his mouth onto her lips, rubbing them until they softened in response. While she was still wanting more of his kiss, Whit moved away. Her gaze followed him as he walked toward the door.

The voice of pride whispered in her ear and advised against standing there and watching him leave. It was too clear an indication of what she was feeling for him. Shari turned to the wrinkled clothes on the bed, and wrapped the towel completely around her. She listened for the click of the door opening to signal his departure. When she heard Whit pause, she sent a side glance in his direction.

He was standing beside the chest of drawers. "While you're choosing what to wear tonight, pick something that will go with this," he ordered, and tossed the ring box across the room onto the bed in front of her.

Her backbone stiffened at his autocratic tone. She stared at the ring box, making no move to pick it up until she heard the door open and close behind Whit.

Nothing had really changed. He had kissed and caressed her—but for his pleasure. He still believed he could tell her they were getting married and she would accept it—he could toss an engagement ring on the bed and she would wear it.

Shari held the ring box in her hand, debating what to do with it. Curiosity briefly overcame her sense of independence. She couldn't resist opening it.

Disappointment pulled down the corners of her mouth. The ring inside was ugly, a single diamond surrounded by a circlet of smaller ones. Yet it looked gaudy and cheap. Whit had picked this out for her to wear? She hadn't realized he had such poor taste.

She snapped the box shut in a gesture of dislike and closed her fingers around it. For the time being, she set it on the nightstand next to her bed. She swore to herself that she'd never be caught dead wearing that *thing*.

Taking the wrinkled clothes from the bed, Shari put them back on a hanger to be pressed another time. Then she went through her closet to find something else to wear that night. It wasn't easy when she'd already made her choice once. Nothing else seemed quite as appropriate. Finally she settled for the simplicity of a pleated white skirt and a tunic blouse in a green and gold print.

The better part of a half hour was gone before Shari was dressed and her makeup was on. She left the room to join the rest of the family downstairs. As she was walking down the steps, Whit came out of the library.

When he saw her, he came to the bottom of the staircase and waited for her. Under his steady gaze, her heart began to beat unevenly, but outwardly, Shari appeared calm.

"Very nice," he remarked when she paused on the last step, her hand resting on the carved banister. His sweeping glance had already indicated that he was referring to the outfit she was wearing yet Shari was disturbed by the sensation that he could see through her clothes.

"It's better than nothing, which was your suggestion," she replied with a hint of challenge.

"A suggestion that I retracted," Whit reminded her that he had decided to keep her nudity for his eyes alone.

He had decided, the phrase burned with the implication that she had no say in the matter. He reached out to curl the fingers of her left hand over his. His glance noticed the bareness of her ring finger and swung sharply to her face.

"You aren't wearing the engagement ring." The statement bordered on a challenge.

"No," Shari admitted freely. "I told you I didn't want it. You seem to be the one who's engaged because I'm certainly not. Maybe you should wear it."

He tipped his head to the side to regard her with narrowed eyes. "What was all that talk about children and grandchildren?"

"You brought the subject up," she reminded him smoothly. "I only corrected you when you were talking about grandchildren before there were any children. Perhaps I should have added before there was any marriage."

"You still claim that you don't want to marry me after that little scene upstairs?" Whit murmured with dangerous softness.

"I don't see that marriage has anything to do with what happened," Shari reasoned with wide, mocking eyes. "If you recall, I admitted that you would be an ideal lover. I didn't say anything about a husband." His features hardened at her barely veiled taunt. She smiled with more mockery. "Why do you look so grim? Did I say something wrong?"

"I will be the only lover that you'll ever know. And I'll be your husband as well," he stated tersely.

"I did say the wrong thing, didn't I?" She released a low, throaty laugh. "I forgot you Lancasters always want sole ownership. You don't believe in sharing."

"Neither do you," Whit countered with a flint-hard smile.

Shari changed the subject rather than argue that point, because she had already experienced jealousy where he was concerned. But she didn't want him to know that.

"I suppose you conveniently avoided talking to my mother about this myth you are trying to perpetuate," she charged.

"It isn't a myth, Shari," he corrected blandly. "You are going to marry me whether or not you choose to wear an engagement ring at this particular point. So Elizabeth isn't under the wrong impression when she believes that. You might as well accept it."

"Nobody decides anything for me," she stated. "You may think you do, but I assure you that you don't. I do what I want—not what you or Granddad or Mother think I should. You might as well accept that."

"I do accept it." There was a smile in his eyes. "Because I know what you want. It happens to be the same thing I want."

"I wouldn't be too sure about that," Shari retorted, and didn't want to continue the conversation. "I believe the others are in the dining room already. Don't you think it's time we joined them?''

Keeping a hold of her hand, Whit moved to one side so she could descend the last step. His firm grip was a show of possession, a silent declaration that her place was by his side.

Together they entered the dining room, causing all heads to turn their way. The pleased looks on their faces told Shari what they were thinking. It probably appeared very romantic for the, supposedly, engaged couple to walk in hand in hand. She had denied the engagement to everyone there so she didn't waste her breath doing it again.

With a little tug, she was able to pull her hand free from Whit's grasp and walk to the chair where her mother was seated. "It's wonderful to see you sitting at the table with the rest of us again," Shari declared and bent to kiss the roughed cheek.

"All of us here echo that," Frederick Lancaster inserted, inclining his iron-gray head to the woman seated at the opposite end of the table from him.

"It means very much to me to be here," Elizabeth spoke with stiff care and covered Shari's hand resting on the chair's arm. "Especially tonight. I would have hated to miss my daughter's engagement dinner.''

"It is hardly that, Mother," Shari replied.

"Perhaps not officially an engagement dinner," her mother conceded. "But it is a family occasion."

"Having you with us makes it a special occasion," Shari insisted, in her own way trying to keep the emphasis of the fictional engagement.

But her mother was too much of a romantic to permit that. "I've been wanting to see your ring. Will you show it to us?" Then she noticed Shari's ring finger was bare. "Didn't Whit give it to you? I thought that was why you were so late in joining us."

"He gave it to me." Shari could say that in all honesty, since he had refused to take it back.

"Why aren't you wearing it?" her mother frowned.

Shari moved away from the chair to her own, tossing a glance at Whit to let him field that question.

"There were some difficulties getting it on her finger," he replied with a half-truth and pulled out a chair for Shari to sit on.

"That's one way of putting it," she murmured for his ears alone.

"Was it too small?" her mother guessed and cast a sympathetic glance at Shari. "You should have given Whit your ring size."

"He didn't ask," Shari said, fully aware there were many things he hadn't asked her.

"Now you'll have to take it back to the jeweler and have it made larger. That's a shame," Elizabeth sighed with regret. "Do you have it with you?" she asked Whit. "I'd like to see it anyway."

"No, I don't." The answer was accompanied by a slight shake of his head.

Shari saw a ready-made opportunity to trap him into accepting the return of the ring. She wasn't going to let that slip away from her.

"I have it in my room," she declared and pushed her chair back from the table. "I'd better give it back to you so you can have it fixed." She rose quickly. "Excuse me. It will only take a minute to fetch it."

"It can wait until later," Whit insisted, half-rising out of his chair to stop her.

"I might forget." Her smile was mockingly sweet. "And we can't have that. Once I return it to you, it's out of my hands."

With a faint nod of his dark head, Whit acknowledged the superiority of her tactics. The faint glint in his eye seemed to warn her to enjoy her small victory because there would be other battles.

"Don't be too long!" Rory called after her as she walked quickly to the door. "Mrs. Youngblood is going to start serving dinner."

As usual, Rory was concerned about satisfying his never-ending appetite. Shari wasn't interested in taking her time. She rushed up the stairs and down the hallway to her room. The ring box was where she had left it—on the nightstand of her bed. Shari picked it up and hurried out of the room to retrace her steps.

When she entered the dining room, Whit courteously stood up. She was slightly out of breath from her race up and down the stairs but her green eyes were sparkling. She presented him with the ring box before smoothing the back of her skirt to sit in the chair next to his. A green salad had already been dished for her.

"May I see the ring?" her mother requested as Whit started to sit back down.

He hesitated briefly, and Shari wondered if he was aware of the ring's poor quality. It seemed unlikely since he had expected her to wear it. On the other hand, the ring could have excellent gemstones in it. Shari didn't claim to have an eye for such things. The ring just didn't appeal to her.

Without trying to appear too interested in her mother's reaction, Shari covertly watched Whit walk to the end of the table to her mother's chair and show her the ring. Her mother stared at it for a blank instant, then quickly tried to force a polite expression on her face. Her mother had never been very good at hiding her feelings and Shari could tell she didn't think it was attractive at all.

"It's... very nice." She looked up at Whit and tried to smile.

"I thought it suited Shari," he said and closed the ring box to slip it back in his pocket.

"Yes... well, I'm sure she liked it," her mother responded carefully.

"I was very impressed," Shari said without telling whether the impression had been good or bad.

The look Whit slid to her seemed to contain some secret light that she couldn't fathom. She didn't like the sensation that he knew something she didn't. It put them on uneven footing. Her sense of triumph was shaken by this new uneasiness and she wasn't able to enjoy the special meal the housekeeper had prepared.

As usually happened at the dinner table, the conversation became centered on business which excluded Shari and her mother and for the most part, Rory, too. The discussion continued through the coffee following dessert. Mrs. Youngblood went ahead and cleared the table of all but the cups, aware that Frederick Lancaster could sit at the table for hours.

Shari seemed to be the only one who noticed her mother was getting tired. She leaned toward her. "I think it's time you were getting some rest. I'll help you to your room," she volunteered and straightened from her chair before her mother could protest. "Would you excuse us, Granddad?" She politely asked his permission to leave the table.

"Of course." He gave it immediately. "Forgive me, Elizabeth, I didn't consider how tiring this was for you."

"I am a little tired," her mother admitted reluctantly and glanced up at Shari when she came to her chair. "You needn't come up-stairs with me. Nurse Jeffers can help me."

"But I'm already here," Shari reasoned. "Besides, I can read you another chapter of the Christie novel."

"It isn't necessary," her mother declared. "You should be spending the evening with Whit."

"I'm sure Whit understands that, under the circumstances, I'd rather spend the time with you," she countered, and sent Whit a chal-lenging look that dared him to refute her claim, or question her reasons.

"Yes, I quite understand." Dryness rustled through his voice.

CHAPTER NINE

DURING THE next three days, no mention was made of the ring, although there were several references to the supposed engagement by various members of the family. Shari reacted to none of them while she managed to tactfully avoid being alone with Whit, using one pretext or another.

She did it partly out of self-defense, cognizant of how vulnerable she was to his male persuasions but her main thought was to take a stand and not weaken it by protesting too much. Again, Shari used her mother as a shield.

A light knock on the door of her mother's room lifted Shari's gaze from the envelopes she was addressing; responses to the many "get well" wishes her mother had received. She glanced at her mother, sitting in one of the armchairs.

"Yes, come in." Elizabeth granted the caller permission to enter, and quickly removed her reading glasses, too vain to be seen wearing them.

Mrs. Youngblood walked in, balancing a tray in her hands. "I thought you might enjoy some freshly-baked pecan rolls with your coffee this morning."

"I think you're trying to fatten us up," Shari accused with a laugh and appreciatively sniffed the yeasty aroma of warm rolls. "They smell delicious."

"I have some mail for you, too, Mrs. Lancaster," the housekeeper said as she set the tray on the round table next to Elizabeth's chair. "It's beside the cups."

Laying down her pen, Shari left the antique escritoire and walked over to pour the coffee for the two of them while her mother went through the small stack of envelopes. She added a lump of sugar to her mother's cup.

"More letters to answer?" Shari asked and ruefully shook her head. "At this rate, Mother, you're going to need to hire a social secretary to keep up with all your correspondence."

"Everyone has been so thoughtful," was the absent reply as Elizabeth cast a frowning glance at the housekeeper. "There wasn't anything else in the mail for me?"

"No, ma'am." Mrs. Youngblood paused before leaving the room. "Is there anything else you need?"

"No, this is perfect," Elizabeth assured her but Shari caught the faint sigh, nearly lost under the sound of the closing door.

"Is something wrong?" she asked.

"I ordered a bridal book and catalog over the telephone and asked them to rush it here," her mother explained. "They thought I should receive it in a week or less. I was hoping it would be in today's mail."

"I see," Shari murmured and concentrated on stirring the coffee.

"Have you given any thought to the style of wedding gown you'd like?" Elizabeth tipped her head to one side with curious interest.

"No." Simple, straightforward answers had proved to be best.

"So much of the choice depends on the time of year when the wedding takes place," her mother admitted. "Have you and Whit discussed a date at all? This autumn? Or were you considering a winter wedding?''

"Nothing definite has been decided," Shari replied. As far as she was concerned, not even the engagement was definite.

"There is a great deal that has to be done beforehand. It can't be left to the last minute. You and Whit need to sit down and make some plans."

"Yes, Mother." Which really meant nothing.

"Frederick can give you away," Elizabeth began the planning for her. "I imagine you'll want your two friends from college in your bridal party."

"Perhaps." Shari took a bite of the warm pecan roll, its sweet, caramel topping coating her lips. She licked it away and began chewing. "Mmm, Mom, you really have to eat one of these." It was difficult to talk and chew at the same time but she managed it, because she wanted to change the subject. "They are so good."

"You can't even pick out your wedding colors since they should be appropriate to the season," her mother realized with vague dismay.

"Please, will you stop talking about the wedding?" Shari asked with fraying patience. "It's probably going to be a long time away, and a lot of things might happen between now and then."

"Aren't you and Whit getting along?" The concern was instant. "You haven't quarreled again? The two of you used to get along so well together. Sometimes, I had the feeling you worshiped him."

"I was much younger then," Shari replied, aware that she had regarded Whit with a certain adoration when she was growing up.

Perhaps she had been more amenable to taking orders then. But she wasn't about to marry any man who tossed her a ring and informed her they were getting married—even Whit.

"Then you have argued with him?" her mother concluded from Shari's ambiguous statement.

"Mother, you know that Whit never argues," she reminded her dryly.

The knock at the door was a welcome interruption of the conversation. Shari picked up the china cup of coffee to take a sip.

"Yes, come in." Elizabeth repeated her earlier phrase.

This time when the door opened, Whit entered. He was dressed for the fields, wearing a short-sleeved cotton shirt that exposed his tanned and muscled forearms and snug-fitting brown denim pants that were tucked inside his calf-high leather boots, a modernized image of a plantation owner. His wind-rumpled dark hair glinted with gold lights put there by long hours in the sun. All of Shari's normal body actions were suddenly scattered to the wind by the sight of him.

"Whit, this is a pleasant surprise," her mother greeted him with open delight. "We were just talking about you."

"Yes, speak of the devil," Shari murmured to conceal the havoc his presence was creating with her senses.

Whit ignored her comment, but his glance held a hint of mockery. "I thought I'd find Shari with you," he said to immediately establish she was the one he had come to see. "She's been hiding in here with you a lot lately."

"It's not hiding when you know where I am," Shari countered.

"Maybe 'hiding' is the wrong word," he conceded indifferently. "But sometimes I wonder if you're not afraid of me."

"Why should I be afraid of you?" She laughed to show how ridiculous the idea was.

"I don't know," he admitted.

Without knowing why, Shari felt she was on shaky ground. "Would you like a warm pecan roll? Mrs. Youngblood just brought them up." She picked up the plate to offer him one.

"No, thanks. I have to watch my figure," Whit replied facetiously. "I came to tell you that your engagement present has finally arrived."

"My engagement present?" Shari stared at him blankly. He hadn't said anything about it before.

"Yes. Will you come outside and see it?" The tilt of his head was faintly challenging.

Confused by the situation, Shari didn't know what she should do. If she refused with her mother sitting there, a hundred questions would have to be answered. But it was really her curiosity that insisted she had to see what he'd bought for her. After that gaudy engagement ring, she was prepared for just about anything.

"Naturally, I'm going with you to see it," she replied as if her decision had never been in question.

"Come along them," Whit prodded.

The look in his eyes started a wild fluttering in her stomach. Instead of hurrying as she was told, Shari took her time setting the plate of rolls on the tray and removing the napkin from her lap. When she finally stood up, she glanced at her mother and smiled.

"I'll be back in a bit," she promised.

"Don't count on it, Elizabeth," Whit advised and took Shari by the arm to lead her out of the room.

In the hallway outside her mother's room, Shari stopped to obtain an explanation of his parting remark to her mother. She didn't like the sound of it.

"Why did you indicate to Mother that I wouldn't be coming back right away?" Shari confronted him with her question, eyeing him suspiciously.

There continued to be a hint of complacent amusement in his expression. It glinted in his dark eyes and faintly curved the line of his mouth.

"I just have a hunch this will take longer than you think," was all he would say in response.

Whit placed a hand on the small of her back to direct her to the staircase.

The warmth of his touch radiated through her body. It was always like this. She seemed to come truly alive only when she was with him. If things had been different, she probably would have been clinging to him ecstatically at this moment.

"Why do we have to go outside?" she asked, sliding him a glance as they walked down the stairs. "Can't you bring the present inside?"

"I don't think it would be a good idea." A smile lurked at the corners of his mouth but he wouldn't give her any hints.

"I know you didn't buy me a car. I already have one," Shari said, speaking her thoughts aloud. Then she shot him a look of suspicion. "You aren't taking me outside to force an engagement ring on me, are you? Because it won't work. I don't really want it or your present."

"You'll want the present." His confidence was absolute.

Totally confused, Shari couldn't think of a single thing he could have bought her—and especially one that he knew in advance she wanted. At the bottom of the stairs, he guided her to the wide front door.

As they walked outside, a summer wind tangled itself in her black hair. Shari stopped at the top of the steps to push the strands away from her eyes and look around. She saw nothing out of the ordinary, certainly nothing that might be a present.

"Where is it?" She turned to glance at Whit.

"Over there." His hand motioned to her right.

At first she didn't see what he was indicating. His horse, Banner, was standing in the shade of a tree, all saddled and bridled. That wasn't unusual. And Shari certainly didn't think that Whit intended to present his own horse to her as a gift.

The golden chestnut turned its dish-shaped head in the direction of the house and whickered, catching the scent of its master. When it shifted position, Shari noticed a second horse that had been blocked from her view.

For a full second, she stared at the gray gelding, certain she was seeing things. She didn't dare believe what she was seeing, and turned her searching eyes on Whit.

"Is it . . . ?" Her hopes were raised so high, she was afraid to even ask.

A smile spread lazily across his mouth. "It's Rebel," he confirmed.

Her chin started to tremble as her eyes welled with tears. She was too overcome with happiness to say a word. She didn't understand how he had known.

"Aren't you going to say 'hello'?" Whit gently prompted her.

His question released Shari from the immobility that had claimed her. She ran down the steps and across the lawn to the shade tree where the horses were tied. The gray gelding turned its head and snorted, pricking its ears at her approach.

Shari slowed to walk the last few steps to the horse's head. It stretched out its gray-black nose to her, blowing softly. Her smile tightened with emotion as she reached up to scratch the gray forehead. Beneath its pepperd forelock, dark, luminous eyes looked back at her.

"Rebel, it really is you," she whispered and laughed when the gray tried to nip at the sleeve of her blouse. "You haven't changed a bit, you ornery devil."

She shifted her position to stand to one side of his head and stroke the horse's sleek, muscled neck. There was still a part of her that couldn't believe the gelding was back. She wrapped her arms around its neck and pressed her face against its dark mane, not caring if it seemed foolish or childish. A warm, horsey smell filled her senses.

Rebel didn't care much for displays of affection and tossed his head in protest, rattling the bridle bit in his mouth. So many memories crowded into her mind that she couldn't sort them through.

When the gray horse attempted to sidle away from her, Shari loosened the circle of her arms. She couldn't argue against the gelding's feisty spirit that didn't like being held too tightly. The horse was stubborn and headstrong—like her—Whit had said so many times.

"I wouldn't want you any other way, Rebel," Shari murmured and rubbed its wide chest to calm the gelding down.

"Do you think you can remember how to ride that bundle of trouble?" The low question came from behind her.

Shari glanced once at Whit, then moved to untie the reins. A second challenge wasn't required as she looped the reins over the gray's neck.

"If I don't remember, you can pick me up when I fall off," Shari declared with a reckless smile. "You should know how. You've done it enough times."

With one hand gripping the reins and a handful of mane, Shari hopped to reach the stirrup and swung into the saddle. Rebel pulled eagerly at the bit, his iron hooves impatiently beating the ground. Shari held him in check a few seconds longer until she saw that Whit was ready to mount his chestnut horse. Then she relaxed the pressure of the bit. The gray horse didn't need any other encouragement.

Within two strides, the gelding was in a canter and stretching out to increase it to a run. It didn't seem to Shari that she needed to guide the horse. It was racing with its ears pricked forward as if it was eager to revisit the old trails. She let him have his head and the horse picked the open lane to the tobacco fields, the very route they had always used as a starting point.

Another set of hooves pounded the packed ground behind her. Shari glanced over her shoulder and saw that Whit was gaining on them with his flashy chestnut. Out of sheer fun, she turned the ride into a race, urging Rebel faster and laughing at the wind that tried to whip the air from her lungs.

The thunder of racing hooves hammered in her ears, driving its own brand of excitement into her being. The network of farm roads connecting the different fields were alternately sunlit and shaded. Flecks of foam from the gray's lathered neck were thrown back on Shari. The gray's stride wasn't as effortless as it had been starting out.

When she applied pressure on the bit to slow the horse down, Rebel responded without any protest. She brought him down to a trot. His flanks heaved beneath her as the gelding blew out a rolling snort. She patted his wet neck, smiling her pleasure for the wild ride. It was a long time since she had felt this free, all her tension stripped away.

Just ahead of them, a hen pheasant took wing, flying out of the hedgerow lining the dirt lane. The gray horse still had enough energy to shy at the sudden movement. Shari kept her seat in the saddle, a breathless laugh slipping from her throat when the moment had passed.

The chestnut horse drew alongside the gray. "I don't know which of you is crazier," Whit declared. "You or that horse. It's going to be a toss-up whether he breaks a leg before you break your neck."

But he was smiling and that gold sparkle was in his amber eyes. Shari couldn't have taken him seriously even if the reproval had been meant to be. She was in too glorious a mood to let idle warnings spoil it.

"Part of this still doesn't seem real," she admitted on a contented sigh and lifted her gaze to the clear, blue sky overhead. "I almost think I'm dreaming it. But if it's a dream, I don't care."

"It isn't a dream," Whit assured her. "Rebel is yours again."

She believed him because she had never dreamed in sight, sound and sensation before. Creaking saddle leather, jangling metal bits and the clip-clopping of hooves confirmed the sound part of it. Shari could feel the movement of the horse between her legs and her eyes recognized the gray gelding that had taken her on so many wild rides before.

"Thank you." It seemed an inadequate response, but she wasn't able to express how deeply she was moved by the gift.

Both horses settled into a walk. "I had the devil's own time finding him," Whit said. "He's had two more owners since you sold him. You seem to be the only one who appreciates his lawless ways."

"Not lawless," Shari corrected. "Rebel is just independent."

"Okay, independent," he accepted her adjective with a certain dryness. "Now you understand why I told your mother you probably wouldn't be back for a while. I knew you wouldn't be able to resist riding him."

"You were absolutely right," she agreed. Laughter came so easily to her, rolling from her throat without needing much of a reason.

"Did you tell anyone what you were doing? Have they been keeping it a secret from me?"

"Only Granddad, since he took some of the telephone messages for me," Whit explained. "I wanted to surprise you."

"You succeeded." It was an understatement. Shari leaned forward in the saddle to stroke the gray's neck, almost needing the reassurance of touching the animal.

A pickup truck was parked at a field gate just ahead of them. When they reached it, Whit reined his chestnut aside to talk to the man out checking the field's crop. Shari halted her horse as well, but didn't join the two men.

Her gaze swept the rows of tobacco plants beyond the fence. It was nearly head-high. By late August, it would grow that tall. From her early years of being raised on the tobacco farm, Shari knew the process that was followed.

All during the growing season, the tobacco rows were walked. The pink and white blossoms that bloomed at the top of the plant were cut off, and any suckers that grew were broken off in an effort to keep the plants from becoming leggy. The better grade of tobacco leaves grew close to the ground.

Come September, the burley would be ready for cutting. Field hands would move up and down the rows, cutting leaf by leaf. Then they'd be stacked in the barn for curing. Shari fondly recalled the times just before auctions when Frederick Lancaster used to pace the barns, praying aloud for a damp, piercing cold to finish the curing process.

Whenever she could, she had attended the auctions with Whit. Harvest times were always so festive with Christmas just around the corner. It almost seemed like a county fair, there was so much excitement going on at the auctions. In the three years she'd been away at college, Shari realized she had missed these simple pleasures.

"You're far away." Whit's quiet voice penetrated her reminiscent thoughts, bringing her back to the present.

She darted a brief glance at him and nodded, turning her gaze back to the golding green tobacco fields. "I guess I was," she admitted.

"What were you thinking about?" His gaze studied her with interest as the chestnut shifted beneath him, stamping at a pesky fly.

"Just...that I've missed this." It was a simple answer, but it covered it all.

"I think you've finally come home," he remarked cryptically and lifted the reins. "Shall we head back? It's nearly noon."

"Already?" It didn't seem possible so much time had passed.

"Yes, already," Whit confirmed with a half-mocking smile.

They rode back to the stables at a much slower pace, letting the horses cool off. There was little conversation along the way. Shari relaxed still more, listening to the bird songs and smelling the many scents in the fresh air.

Outside the stable doors, they reined in the horses and dismounted. Shari was conscious of her stiffening muscles, unaccustomed to riding after all this time. When the groom came to lead the horses inside their stalls and unsaddle them, she curved an arm under the gray's neck in a last gesture of affection.

"Why is Rebel getting all the hugs?" Whit asked. "I'm the one responsible for him being here or have you overlooked that?"

"No." She laughed and moved aside so the groom could lead the gelding away.

When she turned to Whit, she experienced a rush of emotion that wasn't limited to gratitude. The only outlet to express it seemed to be a physical one. Shari crossed the small space between them and tightly wound her arms around his middle to hug him. His arms circled her in response as she rested her cheek against his broad chest.

"What made you buy Rebel back for me?" It was something she didn't understand. And she wanted to, because his answer could mean so much—if it was the right one.

"It isn't natural the way you've been shutting yourself in the house lately. I had to find a way to get you out," he replied. "I wasn't sure buying you just any horse would do it. But I knew you wouldn't be able to resist if the horse was Rebel."

"You were right," Shari agreed. It was so easy to enjoy the warmth of his arms without the need to feel on guard.

His head was bent close to her hair. She could feel his breath stirring the black, wind-tousled strands. "Happy?" he murmured.

"Yes." She raised her head to look up at him, her gaze moving warmly over his handsomely male features. "I've never been happier in my life."

Whit combed his fingers into her hair to hold the side of her face in his palm. "Do you still doubt that I could make you happy?"

"You . . . could make me very happy," she admitted, but she knew he hadn't yet. A quiver of unease ran through her nerves. "Did you buy Rebel to try to bribe me into marrying you?" she demanded warily.

"I don't have any doubt that you'll marry me," he stated.

Bitter tears stung the back of her eyes. How could anyone be so thoughtful yet be so arrogant? Yet she didn't try to avoid the kiss when his mouth lowered onto hers. Mentally, Shari could resist his persuasions, but her flesh was too susceptible to his experienced kisses.

His passion remained checked by the publicness of their embrace in the middle of the stable yard. But Whit continued to hold her within the circle of his arms after the kiss was over.

"I know you, Shari," he said, looking deeply into her eyes and seeing the conflicting emotions. "And I know what you want."

"No, you don't," she denied. "You keep *telling* me you do...just as you keep *telling* me what I'm going to do. You're wrong."

"You are stubborn," Whit declared with a trace of grimness.

Her hands pushed at his waist. "Lunch will be ready." She used that as an excuse to break off the embrace. "They'll be waiting for us."

"Yes, we'd better go to the house," he agreed and watched her with a certain closeness after he'd let her go.

On the way back to the pillared house, he didn't hold her hand, or make any attempt to physically direct her course. They were nearly to the steps when Rory intercepted them.

"Was I seeing things?" He directed his puzzled glance to each of them. "I could have sworn I saw Shari riding a gray horse that looked just like Rebel."

"It was Rebel," Whit informed him.

"It was?" Rory's frown deepened. "But where did he come from?"

"Rebel is my engagement present to Shari," he explained.

"Does that mean you really are engaged to
him?" Rory asked her.

"Not as far as I'm concerned," she replied
stiffly and climbed the front steps ahead of
them.

CHAPTER TEN

HER SPOON chased the strawberries in their pool of rich cream, not catching any. Shari didn't really care. She hadn't had a taste for them or any of the dinner that had preceded dessert. A feeling of futility continued to plague her as it had all afternoon. Neither her vigorous protests nor her silences had seemed to make any impression on Whit. He hadn't backed down an inch from his stand that she would marry him, not even relenting so little as to ask her.

"You are very quiet tonight, Shari," her mother remarked with concern. "Is anything wrong?"

"No," she lied, aware of the sweep of Whit's inspecting glance. "I'm just tired I guess."

She gave up any pretense of finishing her dessert and set her spoon on the bowl's serving plate. Taking the napkin from her lap, Shari dabbed the corners of her mouth.

"Aren't you going to eat any more?" her mother protested. "Strawberries and cream are one of your favorites."

"I can't help it if I'm not hungry," Shari insisted, her frayed nerves giving a trace of sharpness to her answer.

"If you don't want the rest of them, I'll take them," Rory volunteered.

"Be my guest." She laid the spoon aside and passed the bowl across the table to Rory.

"I don't know where you put all that food, Rory." Elizabeth shook her head in vague bewilderment. "You have your father's appetite."

Whit wasn't interested in Rory's bottomless hunger. Shari had his full attention. "After your ride this morning, I expected you to be ravenous. You barely touched your lunch, and you left half your dinner."

"What does that mean?" She was irritated with his constant orders and didn't try to hide it from the others. "That you will do the talking and I will do the listening? That's usually the way it turns out with you."

"Shari." Her mother was shocked by her rudeness. "You shouldn't speak to Whit like that."

"I can't be like you," Shari flashed. "I can't be meek and simpering, bowing to his every wish."

"The shock would kill me if you were," Whit offered dryly.

"In that case, maybe I should try it," she threatened. Her hand was doubled into a fist as she tried to twist out of his grasp. "If you don't mind, I'd like to leave the table. We can have 'your' talk in the living room, since you seem to think it's so important. I'll wait for you there—and by all means, take your time about joining me."

Her voice dripped with sarcasm, but she couldn't keep the hurt bottled up inside her anymore. His mouth thinned into a grim line as he let her go. Shari didn't waste time making her excuses to the others at the table. She left the room with her head held unnaturally high.

In the formal living room, she sank immediately onto the plush cushions of the china blue sofa and lowered her head to her hands.

She was trembling, too agitated to sit still. Within seconds, she was up, pacing the floor.

When she heard the approaching footsteps and recognized them as belonging to Whit, Shari turned to face the door. Tension electrified every inch of her until she wanted to scream. Hardly any time had passed since she'd left the dining room, yet he was here already.

Whit paused inside the arched doorway and quietly studied her. Shari was tired of always being on the defensive with him. It constantly put her at a disadvantage.

"I told you there wasn't any need to hurry," she flashed. "Did you think I was going to run away?"

"You've been known to do that when things aren't going the way you want," he replied without any sign of anger.

"That isn't true." Shari was angry, because she was again put in the position of defending her actions.

"You ran off to college when Granddad wouldn't give in to your wishes," he reminded her. "I had to come and drag you back or have you forgotten that?"

"I hadn't forgotten." She didn't want to discuss it. "I wasn't running away."

"What do you call it then?" Whit challenged and came further into the room. "I'd be interested to hear your description of it."

"It doesn't matter," she countered with an irritated shrug. "That happened three years ago. It's water under the bridge now."

"What about a few weeks ago when you allowed your mother to believe you were vacationing with friends on the Coast? You were actually staying at the condominium. I had to bring you back from there, too."

"Is this what you wanted to talk to me about?" she demanded.

"No." He took a deep breath as if preparing himself for the real battle. "I think it's time we cleared up this business about our engagement."

Shari stared at him for a stunned instant. Her laugh was a short brittle sound. "I've been trying to do that ever since you made that ridiculous announcement," she declared. "Don't tell me that you are finally listening to me?"

"Something has been eating at you and I want to know what it is," Whit stated, completely ignoring her caustic response.

His demand to know what was bothering her caught Shari by surprise. She turned away and blinked back the tears that misted in her green eyes.

"I don't understand you, Whit Lancaster." Her voice was low and husky. "Sometimes you can be so wonderful—and the next minute you're acting like a dictator. I wish you could have heard yourself just now."

"Why?" The carpet only partially muffled the sound of his footsteps coming closer to where she was standing.

"Because you weren't *asking* me to tell you—you were ordering me!" Her voice broke and she had to close her mouth to keep from betraying herself.

"And no man is going to order you to do anything." Whit finished the thought for her. "I had a feeling that was it."

She turned on him, hurt and angry that he could dismiss it so lightly. "Then why do you keep doing it?"

"I suppose I do it because I love you." His mouth was twisted in a crooked smile, his voice warm and gentle.

Her heart leaped into her throat at his admission. "That's the craziest reason I've ever heard," she insisted tightly while her gaze wildly searched his expression to make sure he meant it.

"It isn't so crazy, not really," Whit replied. "You have to take into consideration the woman I've fallen in love with in order for it to make sense."

"Who? Me?" A frown of confusion gathered on her forehead. "Why am I to blame?"

"That's because you don't truly realize what I've gone through." His hands curved themselves to her waist and applied pressure to edge her closer to him. "First I had a lot of lusting thoughts to contend with when you were determined to treat me like a brother. Then you ran off to the university and threatened never to come back."

"I didn't really mean that," Shari explained. "Granddad just made it so impossible."

"But I couldn't take the chance that you might have meant it," Whit explained with a

ruing smile. "That's why I came that weekend to bring you home. I couldn't stand the
thought of you not being a part of my life,
however small. A few weekends a year was
better than nothing."

"I thought you wanted me back only because of the family," she admitted, absently
bringing her hands up to rest against his chest.
His heart beat solidly beneath her fingers, the
muscled expanse firm to her touch.

"What other reason could I give?" he
countered, and Shari had no answer for that.
"I wanted you to feel that you were a part of
it—as my wife. I wanted you to feel that you
belonged here at Gold Leaf, so part of my
reason was based on truth."

Looking back, it was all so confusing trying to sort out what had been said from what
had been meant. She still wasn't sure that he
knew the difference between loving someone
and wanting to possess them.

"You don't know how many times I wanted
to go to that university and bring you home
for good." The faint hardness in his eyes
backed up his statement. "It was hell wondering about the men you were dating and
whether you loved any of them."

"I didn't," she assured him. "A couple of times, I thought I might be close but it didn't happen."

"But I didn't know that," Whit reminded her. "After meeting your man-hungry friend, Doré, I wasn't exactly reassured about the company you'd been keeping."

"Doré does come on strong with guys. She came on to you." Shari studied his expression, waiting for some kind of reaction. "You didn't seem to mind."

"I noticed," he admitted. "But I was too busy trying to keep my hands off of you. You weren't exactly making it easy for me either—with all your sisterly hugs and big-eyed looks." He took a hand away to reach inside his pocket. "Which reminds me. I have something to give you."

Shari recognized the ring box. It was the same one she had given back to him. She nibbled at the inside of her lip, nervously wondering how she could tactfully refuse the ring without letting him know how much she detested it.

"Maybe you shouldn't give it to me just yet," she suggested.

"Why not?" His head was tipped downward to give him a better view of her face. "I thought you liked it."

"It isn't that, exactly," Shari hedged, but Whit forced the ring box into her hand. She held it uncertainly.

"Will you open it?" he prompted.

He had actually *asked* her! After all this time she'd spent waiting for him to say something like that, she couldn't very well refuse him.

His hands remained loosely on her waist while Shari braced herself for the sight of that awful ring. Something green winked at her when she opened it. Surprise splintered through her. Instead of the cheap-looking diamond engagement ring, the velvet-lined box contained a square-cut emerald ring flanked by a pair of small diamonds.

Her glance flew to his face, seeking an explanation. "This isn't the same ring," she murmured.

"I should hope not." Whit was trying very hard not to smile, but amusement was running through his entire expression. "The other one was a little costume piece I picked up in a dime store."

"A dime store?" Shari didn't know whether she should laugh or be offended.

"This is the ring I intended you to wear all along," he added.

"Then why did you give me the other one?" Her frown deepened.

"You were so angry when I told Granddad that you and I were going to get married, I wouldn't have been surprised if you had flushed the ring down the toilet—or thrown it in the trash." His smile became more pronounced, and it began to do disturbing things to her.

"I was nearly angry enough to do that," she admitted. "Especially when you tossed me the ring."

"I was afraid to get too close," he mocked.

"Liar," Shari reproved and slanted him a look. "You've never been afraid of anything."

"You're wrong." His expression became very serious. "I was afraid of losing you. That's why I held on so tightly." She felt like melting into his arms at that statement. "You were right when you accused me of wanting sole possession of you."

"Don't you now?" Her voice was barely above a whisper as Shari held her breath.

"Not in the same way," he replied. "I finally recognized that today when I watched you and Rebel together. And after the ride, you got your message across, too, about the way I was *telling* you everything."

"Do you mean it?" She wanted to believe that he finally understood.

"Let's put it this way," Whit suggested and brought her closer, the muscled columns of his thighs pressing against her length. "I'm telling you that we're going to be married." Her heart sank a little at the repeat of that same phrase. "But—I'm also asking you if you'll be my wife."

"Are you just going through the motions of asking me?" Shari needed to be convinced. "Because if you're just saying it to get me to wear this ring—"

"Will you marry me?" he interrupted her to formally propose.

"Yes." Happiness bubbled through her now that she was freely allowed to agree, not hampered by pride or stubborn streaks of independence.

At first, Shari couldn't understand why he had let her go until Whit took the ring box from her and removed the emerald ring from its velvet bed. She was trembling a little when she offered him her left hand so he could slip the ring on. It fit perfectly.

"It's beautiful," she whispered, and meant it.

"It looks as if it had been made just for you," Whit agreed.

When she finally was able to take her dazzled eyes off the ring, Shari lifted her gaze to his face. Love radiated from her like a fire. She held nothing back.

A faint groan came from him before he crushed her into his arms and bruised her lips with his hungry kiss. Her arms were around his neck, the wonderful weight of his ring on her finger.

All the pain and soul-searching resistance had been worth it. He not only desired her, but he loved and respected her, too. Whit was all the man she had believed him to be— strong and gentle, forceful and gallant.

"I love you," Shari declared, running her lips over his smooth jawline.

"You took your time telling me," he complained mildly.

"I have a confession to make," she admitted.

He drew his head back to look at her. "What is it?"

"I was jealous of Doré. At the time, I couldn't understand it because I was still trying to think of you as my big brother. Only..." she paused a second to peer at him through her lashes.

"Only what?" His interest was captured and he wanted to hear more.

"—only I was already starting to notice how sexy you were," Shari finished her sentence with a faintly complacent smile.

"Was that the reason for those looks I was getting?" Whit asked.

"Probably." She remembered the growing fascination she'd felt, but so much had happened afterward, she couldn't recall exactly.

The sound of someone loudly clearing his throat attracted their attention, as it was meant to do. Neither of them felt any guilt about being seen wrapped up in each other's arms, their heads close together. They looked toward the archway, only slightly changing their positions. Frederick Lancaster was leaning on his cane with her mother standing uncertainly beside him.

"May we come in?" the elder Lancaster inquired. "Or is our entrance a bit premature?"

"Come in," Whit invited, taking one arm from around her while keeping the other one around her waist.

"Are you sure it's all right?" Her mother continued to hesitate.

"It's all right," Shari added her assurance—and a carrot. "I want you to see my ring."

"Whit got it back from the jeweler's," her mother guessed and came forward to dutifully admire it. Her reaction was nearly the same as Shari's. "It isn't the same ring?"

"No," Shari admitted and moved her fingers so the emerald gem caught and reflected the light. "It's a long story."

"It's beautiful." Her mother was curious about the story, but she was too polite to ask.

"May I see it?" Frederick Lancaster looked almost humble as he made his request, standing back and not forcing his company on them.

Shari thought he appeared older, and weaker. There was a vulnerable quality about him that she hadn't noticed before. Even the request seemed out of character.

"Of course, you can, Granddad." Her voice took on a gentle tone as she held out her hand for him to view the ring.

Slowly he limped forward. His hand shook a little as he loosely held her fingers. "It's good to see it there," he said gruffly.

"I haven't told her, Granddad," Whit said.

"Told me what?" Her questioning glance was warmly curious.

"The ring—" Granddad Lancaster began, and paused to look at her. Moisture glistened in his eyes. "It was my wife's engagement ring. I had intended all along to give it to you, Shari, but you ran off to college. So I gave it to Whit with the understanding it would be used as an engagement ring for his future bride. Little did I guess that you would be wearing it anyway."

"I didn't realize." The ring had more significance than she had known. It was a Lancaster family heirloom as well.

"I don't believe I have ever told you, Shari, but you look very much like my late wife—

God rest her soul. She was very beautiful." The compliment from the Lancaster patriarch was unexpected. "You remind me of her." A sudden smile touched his mouth. "She was sassy just like you are, too."

"How else could she live with someone like you?" Shari teased and warmly kissed his cheek.

Over his shoulder, Shari noticed Rory standing in the doorway, an eyebrow arched curiously. "What's going on? Are you engaged again?"

"We certainly are," she confirmed.

"I think I'll wait until tomorrow to offer my congratulations. It might not last," he declared.

Whit hugged Shari close to his side, looking down at her. "It's going to last." It was a promise.